T0165370

Rebel in Paradise

Rebel in Paradise

Luis L. Crespo

iUniverse, Inc.
New York   Bloomington

Rebel in Paradise

Copyright © 2009 by Luis L. Crespo

All rights reserved. No part of this book may be used or reproduced by any means, graphic, electronic, or mechanical, including photocopying, recording, taping or by any information storage retrieval system without the written permission of the publisher except in the case of brief quotations embodied in critical articles and reviews.

iUniverse books may be ordered through booksellers or by contacting:

iUniverse
1663 Liberty Drive
Bloomington, IN 47403
www.iuniverse.com
1-800-Authors (1-800-288-4677)

Because of the dynamic nature of the Internet, any Web addresses or links contained in this book may have changed since publication and may no longer be valid. This is a work of fiction. All of the characters, names, incidents, organizations, and dialogue in this novel are either the products of the author's imagination or are used fictitiously.

ISBN: 978-1-4401-6876-5 (pbk)
ISBN: 978-1-4401-6877-2 (ebk)

Printed in the United States of America

iUniverse rev. date: 10/7/2009

Dedication

In memory of Grandfather Elias Vazquez Jabega, Educator, Journalist who I never met.

CONTENTS

ACKNOWLEDGMENT

My appreciation to my family for their patience during the shaking process of writing, with special thanks to my son Luis L. Jr. and granddaughter Sarah E. for the great assistance during the revision and electronic remittance of the edited manuscript. Thanks.

Boston

To walk on Boston's cobblestone streets was entertainment for the young man named Gabriel. The hard but somehow comfortable surface gave him an amusing sensation, even though this was not the first time he'd been in a big city; he had already visited New York on this business trip. But being an outsider, everything caught his attention. The street ended in a wide, open road with heavy traffic, single houses with advertisements on their fronts, changing the ambiance of the neighborhood.

Gabriel crossed the street avoiding the people, carriages, and wagons. Reading the advertisements, he kept walking, gazing at the harbor through the open spaces between the buildings. The pleasant smell of the sea came to him. Shortly, he saw a sign:

Dumont & Fitzgerald
Wharfs—Shipping

He took a paper from his jacket pocket and read the note. He was at the right address; the name posted on the building confirmed it. Gabriel opened the door under the sign and stepped inside to find himself in a large room. To the left he saw a man and a woman in an office separated from the entrance hall by a balustrade.

"Sir, may I help you?" The male employee said standing up.

"Good morning. My name is Gabriel Gilbert. I'd like to see Mr. Dumont."

"One moment, please." The employee went down to the end of the hall then stopped at a closed door. Turning to the visitor, he asked, "You said your name was Mr. Gilbert?"

"Yes."

"I'll be right back."

The employee opened the door, entered and closed it after him. Gabriel looked around. *A woman working in an office?* he thought. In his native state, where slavery was widespread, it was rare to see such a thing.

The male employee came back. Holding the door ajar, he said, "Mr. Dumont is waiting you. Come in, please."

Gabriel walked toward the man. As he did, the front door was opened and a young woman walked in. The female employee stood, greeting the visitor. Gabriel gazed at the women as he reached the office and stepped inside. The male employee returned to his desk and sat, pretending to look at his documents, though his eyes were actually on the two women.

A middle-aged man stood in front of Gabriel. "Mr. Gilbert, I am Mr. Dumont," the man said, smiling as he closed the door. "Glad to meet you."

"Thanks, Mr. Dumont." Gabriel answered, shaking hands.

"Please, sit. How is Boston treating you?" While speaking, Mr. Dumont went behind an elegant bureau and sat in a comfortable-looking chair. To his left was another fancy desk that was currently unoccupied.

"Very good. This is a pleasant community," Gabriel answered as he sat in a chair facing Mr. Dumont's desk.

"We are very proud of our city. Sometimes we have problems but we manage them."

"Well, every town has its ups and downs," Gabriel answered.

"Yes, that is true."

Gabriel decided to turn the conversation to business. "Did you receive my letter?"

"Of course, Mr. Gilbert. We would like to be your shipping company. What city or states are you interested in shipping to?"

"Actually, Mr. Dumont, I need goods shipped to Europe."

"As it happens, we have a regular fleet to the old continent. We can ship merchandise in not more than twenty-five days."

Gabriel frowned. "Today I cannot give you a shipment schedule."

"I understand. Anyway, you must talk with my partner, Mr. James Fitzgerald. Right now he is taking care of a vessel that departs tomorrow. He can answer any questions you may have; he is very knowledgeable."

"I see." Gabriel said. "Do you know when can I talk to him?"

"He will be tied up today. Do you mind coming back tomorrow morning? I'll make sure he'll be here. Sorry for the inconvenience."

"That's fine. I'll be back tomorrow," Gabriel confirmed. Both men stood up and shook hands while going to the door which Mr. Dumont opened. "Mr. Gilbert, a pleasure to meet you."

Gabriel reciprocated, smiling and nodding. Both men went out the office.

The young woman visitor was still there; Gabriel looked briefly at her on his way out. "Miss, how are you?" Mr. Dumont said, approaching her. "It's been a long time we don't hear from you . . ."

Early that evening Gabriel came down to the hotel's dining room. He chose a table with a view of the still-crowded streets. Many pedestrians passing by glanced at the eaters, some almost stopping. A waiter came and showed Gabriel a bottle of wine, which he accepted. He read the menu and, when the waiter returned, ordered a steak.

He looked outside, fascinated by the passersby. Watching the different personalities had become his favorite pastime. This city, one thing in particular caught his attention: the freedom or more accurately, the self-sufficiency the women of this town showed. He was also struck by the surety people in general seemed to have. It was a great difference from what he was accustomed to seeing in his beloved prairie home. *Are we behind the times, or this city too liberal?* he wondered. He had also noticed some of the females in this room discreetly glancing at him.

"Excuse me."

A young brunette woman, curly hair, hazel eyes, was standing at his table. Her face looked vaguely familiar. He stood up and said, "May I help you?"

"Can I sit, please?" the woman queried.

"Of course."

They both sat and at that moment the waiter came, delivering Gabriel's steamy dish. The lady looked at the steak, and then she rapidly looked up to him.

"Sorry to interrupt your dinner," she said. "I saw you at Mr. Dumont's office."

Ah! So that is why her face is familiar.

"I need to work," she stated out of nowhere. "If you talk to Mr. Dumont, he will listen." Her tone was firm, but with a hint of insecurity. She looked at Gabriel's meal again; obviously, she had not eaten.

"Will you please join me?" Gabriel invited and without waiting for an answer, he called the waiter. The woman, visibly embarrassed, did not respond, her eyes downcast.

The waiter returned. "The lady wishes to order," Gabriel told the man.

"Certainly, sir. Madam?" He handed her a menu, which she went through quickly before deciding on chicken breast with a side salad.

"Wine?" Gabriel offered. When the woman nodded, he filled up her glass. "A toast," he proposed, lifting his glass. "Glad to meet you."

She managed to bring a smile to her face as she took a sip. "You may be thinking ill of me . . . " she said, trailing off.

"Miss, I assure you, nothing negative has come to my mind."

"Thank you. I knew you were a gentleman."

For the first time, they looked straight into each other's eyes with ease. Somehow she was more relaxed now, some burden left aside.

"You have not answered me," the woman said.

"About what?"

"Mr. Dumont."

Gabriel realized that this lady must be in a precarious situation. The waiter came with her meal.

"Good, let us eat." Gabriel cheerfully proposed, wishing to eliminate the somber mood in the air. A second suggestion was not necessary; his companion started to eat right away. After a few quick bites, she declared, "I'm glad I came this way."

Gabriel was amused. Here he was having dinner with a perfect stranger. Well, why should he be surprised? Maybe this was common here.

"This is the best thing that's happened to me lately," the woman said between mouthfuls. "I have not had a decent meal in a long time."

"You look well; it's hard to believe what you say . . . not that I think you're lying."

"I know what you mean. My family was in a good position till my husband and later my father passed away."

Gabriel frowned. "Sorry to hear that."

"He was a doctor, had a respectable reputation. After he died, all was lost. We never talked about money or property; we needed not to. No one could imagine things would happen this way."

Finally the mystery was clearing up. As she spoke, Gabriel became more and more interested in her story.

"After my father's death, an employee from the lawyer's office who handled my father's interests came to my house. He asked me to sign documents in order to legalize, he said, the transfer of my father's properties to me. Instead, *he* received them. He also mortgaged my house and then ran away, nobody knows where."

Gabriel felt sympathy for her. "The lawyers, what did they say?" Gabriel asked.

"They have filed charges against him."

"Still, they can't do anything else?"

"Not that I know of," she answered, distraught.

"You need advice from someone knowledgeable."

"Maybe, but what can I do? I had to face all kind of problems, and so suddenly." Sorrow covered the woman's delicate face. Finished with her meal, she cleansed her lips with a napkin, her eyes still looking down.

"More wine?" Gabriel asked, hoping to cheer her up or eliminate some of the troubled thoughts she had.

"Thanks, but I've had enough."

She kept silent, her unhappy expression changing from one form of frown to another.

"Do you have relatives?" Gabriel asked.

"No. My parents came from England when they were young. Later, their parents died and we lost contact with the family abroad. After mother died father occupied all his time in his profession. Now you know why I need to work. Mr. Dumont is the only one who can help me. I know his family but I don't want to take advantage of our friendship."

"I see. I may do business with him, but how effective my words will be, I don't know."

"He will try to please you since you are a future customer," she insisted.

The man shook his head slightly. "Anyway, I cannot help you."

"Why?"

"We have not been introduced. I do not know your name."

"Oh, my God! Please, forgive me. I am so worried I cannot think straight. My name is Vilma Mullen."

"Glad to meet you, Miss Mullen," Gabriel said courteously, slightly bowing his head.

"And your name?" Vilma questioned him.

"On this enchanting evening, it is my turn to apologize," Gabriel replied, pretending seriousness. They laughed like old friends, eliminating any social rule that might prevent strangers from sharing in each other's confidence.

"Gabriel Gilbert, at your service. I am from the South on a business trip."

"Are you a boatman?"

"No. I am just looking for an agent to ship our cotton production to Europe," Gabriel replied.

Vilma nodded silently during the pause that followed. Then, changing the subject, Gabriel asked, "Would you like dessert?"

"No, thanks." Slowly, she looked around. "Being without a chaperone is not right. Anyway, nothing has been for me lately. If Mr. Dumont does not help me, I do not know what I'll do."

"Did you work before?"

"No. Occasionally, I helped my father. As I said, it never crossed my mind I would be in this situation." Her expression became distressed again.

"How about any friends?" Gabriel suggested.

Vilma stated, "You have them when you are in good position, but never during hard times."

"You're absolutely right," he agreed.

"When married, I had many friends. One month before our first wedding anniversary, he was killed in a boating accident. After that, nothing has gone right for me."

Gabriel nodded gravely. "I will try to help."

"Thank you," Vilma said her expression easing. A friendly atmosphere came to the table, which many around the restaurant were scrutinizing throughout the dinner.

"If you cannot find employment, what will you do?"

"I don't know. Already I have sold everything of value I had and hope the bank will give me more time to pay them. I have no other place to live, and recuperating any of what the man from the lawyer's office stole, I've been told, is very unlikely."

Gabriel was impressed. How many women had experienced such situation and overcome it? He'd never known of a similar case. Women in the South were different, it seemed to him. At home, they were maybe not as gay or independent as in this part of the country, a condition that allowed for such troubles as this young, beautiful woman was facing but there they did have a more secure future, as far as he knew. Anyway, he had decided to try to help this lady in distress.

"To get hired will be difficult. If you let me, though, maybe I can solve your problems," he comforted Vilma.

"Nobody can!" She released undeniably authentic tears, her voice full of despair.

The next morning, Gabriel walked into Mr. Dumont's place of business. He was rapidly escorted to the private office. "So sorry I'm late," he apologized.

Mr. Dumont greeted him, waving off the apology, and introduced his partner, Mr. James Fitzgerald. After shaking hands, the man invited Gabriel to sit.

"Francis told me you are looking for a shipping port," Mr. Fitzgerald said, getting right to business.

"That is correct."

Mr. Dumont sat behind the bureau on the right, Mr. Fitzgerald on top of the one to the left, facing Gabriel. "We offer shipping service for all kinds of merchandise," Mr. Fitzgerald explained. "You probably know our bay is one of the busiest in the region. Even so, we can accurately predict dates of departure and arrival of our vessels. Mr. Gilbert, how often do you ship your product?"

"I don't have a schedule right now, but we will notify you of shipments well in advance," the prospective client promised.

The office clerk knocked twice on the door and came in, followed by a presentably dressed black man.

"Excuse me, Mr. Dumont. John brought the papers you requested," the employee said. On his way to Mr. Dumont, the black man took a rapid glance at Gabriel. "Sir, the documents from Pier Three," he informed, handing an envelope.

"Thanks, John," Mr. Dumont said to him.

He and the clerk left; Gabriel and the black man exchanged a quick look.

"Mr. Dumont, who is this black man?" Gabriel asked with a note of curiosity.

"Him? He's John."

"Is he your employee?"

"Not exactly, Mr. Gilbert. Occasionally he does errands for us."

"I may be wrong . . . " Gabriel started.

Mr. Dumont and his partner looked at each other, surprised by Gabriel's inquiry.

"John is a reliable man, always handy," Mr. Fitzgerald explained. "Nobody's ever complained about him and let me tell you, many people around here use his services."

Gabriel said, "I see you have a good opinion of him."

"If you know anything we would like to hear it," Mr. Dumont expressed.

"That man is a maroon, a runaway slave of a friend of mine," Gabriel informed them.

This news, though not pleasant, gave the associates some relief. After all, being called a 'maroon' was not a serious matter to be accused of; at least, by Northern standards.

"John is from Lower Canada, if I remember correctly," Mr. Dumont explained. "He has manners, no slave."

Gabriel smiled. These respectable gentlemen, although close geographically, were so far from the world of the South. But to argue would not be appropriate.

"When did this 'slave' escape?" Mr. Fitzgerald questioned.

"Maybe five, six years ago," Gabriel estimated.

"Mr. Gilbert, it could not be John. No time for getting residency in Canada and moving here," Francis Dumont reasoned.

"Maybe. But his face . . . I am certain he is Simon, the runaway slave," Gabriel insisted, even though for the other two, this claim was questionable.

"Well, let us go back to business," Mr. Fitzgerald suggested. "Your trade is cotton, right?"

"That's correct, sir."

"How many bales on each shipment?" Mr. Fitzgerald asked.

"Each time is different; it depends on how the harvest and the weather have been. We don't always get the same results."

"That is understandable. Even so, this information is vital for shipment and delivery."

"I know that, Mr. Fitzgerald," Gabriel responded, adding, "As said before, I'll send the details for each load in advance. You will have enough time to accommodate the merchandise we need to send abroad."

"What ports are using now, Mr. Gilbert?" Mr. Dumont questioned.

"Charleston."

"I know the place," Mr. Fitzgerald said. "Once the ship I was aboard stopped there. Delightful bay. Well, to draft a proposal, we need to know some details."

"I am ready," Gabriel answered. And with that they began drawing up papers.

It was past midday when Gabriel left the office. The meeting was fruitful. The young man had been able to provide much of the business information. However, some of the details would have to be compiled by Gabriel's father. He promised to get those records from Mr. Gilbert as soon as possible.

It was a hot day. The high, bright sun made people and carriages move faster, seeking shade. Gabriel looked at the many well-dressed female strollers, some with umbrellas. He almost stood still when a couple of black women passed by. He shook his head, thinking, *How different they are, what a contrast with . . .* then something caught his attention. *Wait! That black man, is it the runaway slave?*

"You!" Gabriel shouted. The man turned and saw Gabriel, but he went on his way. The young Southerner ran, reached out and grabbed the black man by an arm.

"You are Simon, the runaway slave!"

"Sir, my name is John . . . John Smith!" the man assured nervously.

"No, you are not! I know you very well, Simon."

"Please, you are hurting me!" Shaking, the man tried to release himself from Gabriel's hands. A loud noise interrupted the men's struggle. A carriage had strayed from the street and fallen into a ditch not far from them. The coachman went down, checked the wheel, and tried to pull it out, but could not move it.

"Please, somebody help us!" A beautiful young woman standing in the carriage's door, called for assistance.

"Miss Nell, I'll help you!" John promptly offered; evidently, he knew the lady. Making good use of Gabriel's loosening of his grip at the commotion, the black man untangled himself and ran to the accident. Gabriel, forgetting prejudices, also approached the two men who, despite joining forces, still couldn't release the wheel.

"To take it out," Gabriel said, addressing the coachman, "it is necessary to bring the carriage up. Ask your passenger to step out; it may not be safe to stay there."

The man went to the carriage and explained the situation to the lady, who disembarked from the wagon. She was wearing a wide-brimmed hat that protected her from the sun. Gabriel, going to the rear of the coach, glanced at her. She had big, blue eyes.

Curious-looking pedestrians were standing by. "When I lift the carriage, pull the wheel out," Gabriel instructed the two men.

They agreed. Gabriel, bending on his knees, put both hands on the lower rear end of the coach frame, and then raised it enough for John Smith and the driver to release the wheel from the deep pit. The horse, pushed by the freed carriage, began trotting away. It only got a few yards before the coachman and John ran and stopped it. The passenger girl followed them.

"Thank God you were around, John. Thank you very much," she acknowledged. John smiled at her gratitude as he moved to the other side of the coach, hiding from Gabriel behind the horse. The lady, helped by the coachman, got back into the vehicle. The driver took control of the reins and put the carriage in motion.

"Thank you, sir!" the blue-eyed girl called to Gabriel as they departed.

Soon, the carriage had disappeared in the crowd. Gabriel looked for John, the runaway slave, but he saw no trace of him. He smiled; there was little he could do. *Remember*, he said to himself, *this is not your terrain. This is almost a foreign country.*

Days later, Gabriel came back to Mr. Dumont's office after having received a notice from him. He was promptly led into the private room; by now the employees knew him well. Smiling, Francis Dumont received him. "Glad to see you."

"Likewise. Sadly, I have no news yet. To compile the information requested will take my father a few more days," Gabriel said, sitting on a chair across Mr. Dumont's bureau at his invitation.

"I know, I know. I wanted to see you because the other day, you helped my daughter's carriage. When she described the gentleman helping them, I recognized it was you. Since we know each other, she wishes to thank you personally. She regrets that with the agitation at the moment, she did not do it properly."

So, that beautiful Bostonian is the daughter of this man, Gabriel thought. So far the men had been so busy taking care of business matters that they had not discussed personal things, like family.

"Your daughter? It's a small world," Gabriel said, nodding.

"She can receive you late this afternoon, if you're not busy."

The young man was taken aback. Meeting relatives of persons with whom he had business relations was the last thing he expected. Nonetheless, he said, "I would be delighted to see her today."

"Great! You are not familiar with the city, so I'll send my carriage to pick you up and bring you to my house," Mr. Dumont offered.

The Dumonts' house was in a typical family neighborhood of the outskirts of Boston. Francis Dumont greeted Gabriel openly, as an old friend. He introduced his wife, Mary, a tiny, lovely lady and his daughter, Nell, a slim young woman, neither small nor tall, with blonde hair and big, blue eyes. After the initial greetings, Mary Dumont suggested sitting on a terrace at the back of the mansion overlooking the surroundings.

"Mr. Gilbert, thank you for your kind help," Nell Dumont said once everyone was seated.

"It was a pleasure; after all, it gave me the opportunity to meet you."

Nell blushed slightly.

"Good afternoon, everybody." A young woman entered, saluting with a joyful voice. Nell stood up, went to the visitor, and embraced her.

"Mr. Gilbert, this is my good friend, Susan." Nell presented.

Gabriel stood up and shook hands with the newcomer, returning the greeting. A servant brought a tray with pastries, fruits, a pitcher of lemonade, and glasses, setting it on a nearby table. Mary Dumont went to the table and asked Gabriel what he wanted. Nell came to help.

The reunion went amicably. The Dumonts' friendly behavior eliminated any doubt or restraint one might have with people they'd just met. The presence of Susan, with her spontaneous gestures, contributed to dissipating any new-acquaintance blues.

"Are you staying long in Boston, Mr. Gilbert?" Susan asked.

"I am waiting for information from my business. When I receive them, I will expedite talks with Mr. Fitzgerald and Mr. Dumont. Only then will I'll know when I'll be leaving."

"I am afraid you will be around for some time," Mr. Dumont estimated, frowning. "I am going with my family to our country estate next week. By the time we come back, you'll have received news."

"Do you have friends in the city, Mr. Gilbert?" Nell inquired.

Gabriel gave a slight frown. "No, I don't."

"Mr. Gilbert, how would you like to come with us?" Mr. Dumont offered gallantly.

"Oh, I don't want to be a hindrance," Gabriel replied courteously.

Mr. Dumont waved a hand. "You will not. We always have guests. Susan is coming. If you like the outdoors, this is a great opportunity to get to know New England."

"We would be glad to have you, Mr. Gilbert," Mary Dumont added.

"The coming weeks are hot. People leave the city. There is no other place better than going to the country. But of course, if you prefer to stay . . . " Nell said, coyly not looking at the young man. Gabriel was still seemed hesitant.

"Nell, Mr. Gilbert does not know how bad summer is here," Susan added.

Francis Dumont said, "In reality, there is nothing to do during the next weeks. You'll have no regrets coming to the forest." His wife agreeing.

Gabriel considered for a moment as the room fell silent. Leaving the city was not in his plans. Besides, going to the countryside was something he and his friends did most frequently. But how could he decline such friendly invitation without an honorable reason for staying there, where 'nobody' knew him? Alas, coming to the Dumonts' outing was the obvious decision.

"You win. I will be your guest," Gabriel finally acceded.

"That's wonderful!" Nell exclaimed. "I promise you'll find it enjoyable."

The Dumonts' countryseat was surrounded by small dwellings. Gabriel arrived late in the afternoon. He was accommodated in a cottage not far from the main building, though he did not see his hosts until dinnertime. A servant came and escorted him to the house, where was received with the usual hospitality.

After a pleasant meal, everyone came outside to the garden for a walk, enjoying the fresh evening. Soon, Mr. and Mrs. Dumont sat on a rustic bench along the way. Nell, Susan, and Gabriel continued. The sun, still lingering on the horizon, provided the perfect summer evening invitation to stroll around.

"Mr. Gilbert, what would you like to do?" Susan asked. "We have many attractions. There are picturesque villages, and mountain trails with beautiful views."

"I am a foreigner. You ladies, decide."

"You are free to go where you wish," Nell pointed out. "You are welcome, but do not feel obligated to follow us. You can go to any place you chose."

"We had a great group last year," Susan said, unaware that Gabriel was going to answer Nell.

"True, Susan," Nell agreed. "Mr. Gilbert, how about this? We'll let you know the previous day the places we'll go. Then you decide to come with us or go by yourself."

"That is fair," he said, agreeing.

They came back where the Dumonts sat. "Did these girls bore you, Mr. Gilbert?" Francis asked jokingly.

"No, although maybe I am not the most exciting companion," he responded.

"Please, Mr. Gilbert! That is not true," Nell replied quickly.

"You will get along well," Mary Dumont predicted.

"I ordered to have horses ready tomorrow. We'll go to the stream down toward the town," Francis informed the others.

"Wonderful! We went there last year," Susan reminded them.

"Mr. Gilbert, will you come ride-horse with us?" Nell questioned.

"I am afraid of horses, but I shall be there," he responded with a ceremonial tone, making the group laugh.

"Great," Francis said, standing up. "We are going to be together for the next weeks and we already know each other. Why shall we not call the young man Gabriel?"

"That sounds acceptable to me," he agreed.

"Good! It will be easier for all," Susan promptly assured. And with that they retired to their accommodations for the night.

The ride to the brook turned out to be well worthwhile. Just to look at the pure, clear stream was enough to ease any fatigue from the trip. Nell, Susan, and Gabriel walked along the running water, pausing occasionally, sitting on big rocks alongside the current. The Dumonts preferred to spend more time in one place, while the youngsters moved from one spot to the next, always finding new marvels of nature. Gabriel enjoyed this place. The trees were quite different from those in the South. The freshness emanating from the stream's current relaxed them.

On the way back, the group stopped in the nearby town on the coast. The women visited souvenir shops, boutiques, and all kinds of stores. Francis and Gabriel variably entered or waited outside.

Afterward, Nell, holding hands with Susan, Gabriel at their side, walked down to the nearby beach. They enjoyed the saline air of the sea as they walked slowly because of the sand.

"Gabriel, so far you said very little about you," Susan observed.

"What do you want to know?"

"Let us see . . . for example, what you do in your leisure time"

"Susan, please. Don't be indiscreet."

"I'm not, Nell. We are already friends, no?"

"Well, Susan, I have nothing much exciting to talk about, anyway."

"You can tell us about your family," Nell suggested.

"All right." Gabriel paused, looking for the proper words. "I live with my parents and sister."

"Ah, a sister!"

"Yes, Susan. What is amazing about that?" he questioned.

In the distance, Gabriel saw two women and a man in bathing clothes, lying on the sand close to the water, away from others at the beach. It caught his attention; this was a first for him. He had seen women in bathing clothes via the new marvel called photography, but never in person. He continued, "We have a cotton plantation. My father is thinking of growing tobacco, too." Gabriel kept talking to try to distract the girls' attention from the bathers. Susan gave them a quick look.

"How is your relationship with your sister?" Nell asked, apparently not disturbed by the bathers.

"It's good. Sometimes we disagree, but never over anything important."

This type of social, familiar talk became a commonly part of any daily activity. A genuine comradeship quickly developed among the new friends.

Later, the three young adults agreed to meet for a comedy show at an open theater in the village.

"Sorry," Gabriel apologized, sitting next to Nell as he entered late.

"What happened?" Susan asked, sitting at Nell's other side.

"I forgot the time. Besides, I got confused with the address. Did I miss anything good?"

"The 'British Blond Bombshell' already appeared," Susan answered.

"Shh," Nell interrupted. "The comedian is coming."

A man came onto the open stage, walking slowly from one end to the other, looking at the public. He started saying in a grave tone of voice, "If there is something I have experience with, its *women!*" There were some laughs. "Let me tell you, I have been surrounded by women all my life. Don't believe me? I grew up with *five* sisters!"

With an ample smile, the actor looked straight at the audience. "And *I* was the little one!" More laughs came from the crowd. "My sisters took care of me; I was always with them. When shopping, they'd put dresses on me to see how they looked. Oh, do I have experience with women! Hum!"

The audience laughed loudly. The comedian's constant walking, fiddling with his hat, and rapid gestures complemented his words, creating the perfect ambience to draw spontaneous laughs. "*Five* women! And I am not counting my mother, grandmother, or the aunts, and nieces I grew up with. Oh, if I have experience with women . . . !"

After the performance, the vacationers completed their evening by taking a walk around the village, glancing at cottages and residences along the way while enjoying the perfect weather.

"Gabriel, what's your sister's name?" Nell was interested.

"Her name is Anne."

Nell said, "That's a pretty name. If I had a sister or brother, we would be very close."

The sincerity and warm tone of Nell's voice left no doubt in Gabriel's mind. Day by day, an authentic admiration for this woman gradually developed in the young man.

"Look, Nell, what a beautiful garden!" Susan exclaimed pointing to a big lawn.

"What a great variety of flowers and shrubs," Nell added.

The three friends stood still for a few moments, contemplating the magnificent display of colors arranged in perfect harmony, revealing the owner's good taste and the meticulous work of the gardeners.

"Nell, are your parents feeling well?" Gabriel asked as they continued walking.

"Yes; Mother wanted to relax. Because the theater is open air, she was afraid that maybe the sun would be too hot. It was last year; we nearly swooned. Fortunately, today was nice and breezy. We needed not even use our umbrellas."

The threesome spent other afternoons doing various activities. The next day's tennis match was an indelible experience for Gabriel. Both women insisted playing against him at the same time. Gabriel had not recovered from one shot when another was coming. They laughed and laughed at each volley, Gabriel struggling to keep up. The score? Who cares! Having a good time was all that mattered.

A few days passed leisurely. One day the group took a midday excursion to a lake. The sun was not too hot for the short hike. They stopped at a hut near the water's edge. Francis and Mary Dumont soon sat on beach chairs, not interested in going farther. The youngsters, however, merrily ran along the clear water, admiring stones shaped by the ages. The quiet scenery invited adventure.

Nell proposed to go boating, and Gabriel immediately agreed. They went to the boathouse and rented one. As they started to go aboard, Susan changed her mind. Nell and Gabriel tried to persuade her, but she did not alter her decision. She left the other two alone.

Once on the boat, Gabriel took control of the oars. Nell sat on the stern of the boat and she trailed her fingers through the crystalline water as they rowed. There were no clouds above, making for a peaceful, enchanting moment. Nell started to sing lowly, looking at the water and paying no attention to others going by in their boats. Many of those they passed looked on, admiring and envying the man rowing and his date. Gabriel contemplated that figure in front of him, so graceful and those sky blue eyes that more and more called for his attention. It was a perfect afternoon.

More days passed. Then one day, the heavens opened with a heavy rain. However, this did not stop Gabriel from coming to the Dumonts' residence; it was not so difficult a thing that it could keep him away. To be with the girls, sharing laughs and even the simplest conversation was more pleasant for the young Southerner than staying alone. Susan and Nell were surprised when he showed up, but they soon started playing cards and chatting, paying no mind to the overflowing brooks and rivers outside.

As customary in the season, the next day was a perfect, sunny summer day that allowed them to resume their outside program. Today, it was up to the mountains. The trail was narrow and beautiful. Tall trees provided shadows and the morning breeze made the hard track easy. The first part was covered on horseback. When the terrain became too dangerous, they had to abandon the horses. Francis Dumont instructed a male servant accompanying them to find refuge for the animals and wait there till they come back.

The group continued going on foot. Gabriel commented on the difference between the forest of the South and this region. If there was any unusual thing on the way, Susan noticed and pointed it out. She often made everybody laugh with her somehow childish expressions of wonder and delight. The road got gradually more difficult which proved hard for Mary Dumont. They took a while to sit down in a shaded spot and gain strength for the last trek to the summit.

The wide, magnificent view from the top of the mountains proved to be worthwhile, especially for Gabriel since never before he had the opportunity to view such a panorama. Sitting on the ground, Nell, Susan and Gabriel praised the scenery. Nell affirmed that this was the best, clearest, farthest reaching sight she had seen since visiting this spot and Susan warmly supported her assessment.

"Well, young man, what you think?" Francis said coming from behind joining the onlookers.

"This is really fantastic. I have never seen anything like this," Gabriel testified.

"We told you weeks ago that this would be a journey to remember!" Susan said with her usual, festive tone.

"I'm glad you are not disappointed," Nell added.

"These have been some of the most memorable days of my life," Gabriel confessed smiling broadly at Nell.

"Well, this is our last trip," Francis announced. "Our time is over. We'll return home tomorrow."

"Yes, Father," Nell said standing up. "We have had a great vacation."

Susan and Gabriel stood up as well. Francis, followed by the girls and Gabriel walked to the shaded area where Mary Dumont and a female servant, on a rustic table had set out fruits and refreshments. The youngsters welcomed the snack.

Next day, the morning sun passing through thick clouds gave sufficient light for the Dumonts and friends to enjoy an abundant breakfast in the garden. The vacation had reached its final day. Happily, they swapped stories of their favorite moments still fresh in their memories. No one could believe it was over. Never had time run so fast.

After breakfast, they walked around wishing to stop the passing hours, pushing back their moment of departure. Upon reaching the house's main entrance, Mary and Francis decided to go inside; they needed to take care of few final details. Susan, too, was not through packing her suitcases. Nell and Gabriel continued wandering around, remembering moments they had shared. Gabriel was falling deep in those bright, big blue eyes.

"Nell, I have enjoyed every second we have been together."

"Thank you, Gabriel. On very few vacations I had so many pleasant days."

"Do you come every summer?"

"Yes, we visit different places, according the persons around. This year we came a little late. My father was busy in early summer. You did not meet our neighbors; usually we go on vacation at the same time. This year they went abroad; we didn't have much interest in coming, though. You made a difference in that, too."

"I'm glad you invited me." There was a special tone in Gabriel's voice. He looked firmly at his companion. Nell turned her head to the other side to avoid his penetrating eyes.

"Gabriel!" Francis Dumont yelled, approaching them. John Smith the messenger was there. "John has just arrived with good news. Your father answered."

Those words, weeks before would have made Gabriel very happy but not on this particular day.

"My partner James is checking the information received. He is waiting for me for the final draft of a contract proposal."

The young man frowned. There was Simon, the maroon, with the most untimely notice he could possibly deliver.

"Well, Gabriel, what you say?" Francis questioned the indecisive man. John stood a little far away.

"Sure, I will take care of that," Gabriel finally answered.

"Great!" Francis said. "Your coach will leave late this morning. We can meet the day after tomorrow in my office."

"I will be there, Mr. Dumont."

Francis turned to his daughter. "Nell, your mother was looking for you."

"All of my things are taken care of; let me see what she wants," Nell said walking to the house, followed by her father and John. Gabriel watched as they walked away. Something inside him was departing too. He went to his cabin and arranged his luggage in haste. He felt mad without knowing why.

Shortly, the Dumonts were ready to depart. Gabriel got closer to their waiting carriage. Francis and Mary came out the main building and said good-bye to their guest. Susan and Nell walked out. Susan shook hands with him and kept going. Nell smiled at Gabriel.

"This has been a joyful vacation . . . You are a nice person," she said, a bit awkward.

He wanted to answer, but no sound came. A rare feeling went through his body. She was leaving . . . meaning no more going out . . . seeing her . . . talking to . . . laughing with . . . that was impossible! He could not allow that to happen.

"Marry me!" More than words, it was a desperate, last-minute cry.

Nell stopped smiling, stunned by the unexpected proposition. Recovering, a broad smile spread across her lovely face.

"Yes!" she answered.

"Nell, we are waiting!" Mary Dumont called. Nell walked to the coach and got into it, still smiling. The carriage pulled away. A hand stuck out of the horse-drawn vehicle and waved. Gabriel, moving both arms, answered her farewell.

A nervous Gabriel knocked on the door. It was still early morning, but his impatience had not let him to wait. A young female servant opened the door. Gabriel requested to see Mr. Dumont and Nell too. The woman invited him to come in.

Gabriel paced from one end of the entrance hall to the other, his eyes constantly checking the open door connecting to the room where the servant went. He could not sit as suggested by the house worker, could not relax and be quiet. The trip back to the city had been wearisome, not because of the distance but his fears. His thoughts raced. *What does she think of me? Did she really mean yes? Will she take me seriously or think that was a joke?* That last idea dampened his spirit. No, he rejected it. She could not take his words so lightly, and she must know his feelings were legitimate, sincere. And her parents, had she told them? Ever since he asked her, his brain had been working, telling him a thousand things he should have done. Who, in his sane judgment, would do this?

Mr. Dumont finally came and shook hands with Gabriel. Then the appearance of a smiling Nell, followed by her mother, made Gabriel rush to her offering his hands. For the first time, they held each other firmly, putting an end to Gabriel's worries. Francis, embracing his wife by her shoulders, looked at the couple who had eyes only for each other. It took more than one suggestion by Mary and Francis for the sweethearts to follow them to the living room and sit down.

Gabriel was all speech, explaining to his future parents-in-law how sorry he was that he had not told them in the country. In Nell he had found what his life was lacking. Now he was so happy. Mary excused herself and Francis told Gabriel he was welcome, to see Nell happy was wonderful. Mary came back followed by a servant carrying a tray, a bottle of wine and glasses.

"This occasion is worthy of a toast," Mary said. Francis filled the glasses and gave one to each person. All drank while the joyous father expressed his best, warm wishes to the couple.

Nell and Gabriel's engagement developed without difficulty. From the first day the Dumonts had opened their arms, no obstacles stood in their way. Gabriel and Nell, holding hands walked around the house, in the garden, everywhere, exchanging lovers' phrases, expressing the profound feelings their hearts felt. They became inseparable; they could not be one without the other, bringing the romance to its highest level. Nothing but happiness had a place in their world. Whenever Mr. Dumont got near Gabriel to remind him that there was a business the young man had forgotten, he had no opportunity to initiate a conversation beyond a warm, friendly salutation that distracted the point he'd meant to bring up.

As the days went by, Gabriel eventually realized he was running out of time. After bringing it up with Nell, he requested the presence of her parents.

"You have been so kind to me," Gabriel stated.

"I am glad you gave us this opportunity," Francis promptly intervened. "We are thrilled you want to marry our daughter; to see her happy is our major desire."

Gabriel smiled at his fiancée and he brought up the purpose of this meeting. "As you know, I am not from Boston. Nell and I would like to prolong our engagement, but I have been here too long already; I can't stay much longer. Therefore, if you give your permission, we would like to marry as soon as possible."

"How soon?" a worried Mary Dumont asked.

"We don't know . . . a month, maybe. When everything is ready," Nell answered rapidly.

A complete silence filled the elegant room. Gabriel and Nell, holding hands, waited. The good news was, in a way, difficult for the loving parents.

"Where do you plan to live?" Mr. Dumont asked tentatively.

"In my parents' estate at Roseville. The mansion is big enough," the suitor explained.

Facing reality, Francis mustered the courage to ask, "When will you go south?"

"After the wedding, of course," Gabriel answered.

"I promise will write and visit frequently," Nell pledged, trying to dissipate her parents' fear and her own because they had never been separated.

Mary looked anxious. Francis said, "Gabriel, the shipment contract. We never discussed it." The new subject eased the atmosphere slightly.

The young man put a hand to his forehead. "Sorry, I completely forgot."

"My partner James and I wrote a draft with the most generous commercial terms for both parties," Francis explained.

"Tomorrow morning I'll go to your office," Gabriel promised. "Anyway, the final decision is upon my father. I will mail the contract proposal and he will answer as soon as possible."

Another long silence followed. Francis Dumont looked at his wife, who lowered her eyes, avoided his.

"Well? You did not answer about the wedding," Nell put forth again the main question.

"I never imagined things would happen this way." Mary said almost crying.

"Neither did I, Mother."

After a pause, Mr. Dumont announced: "You have our blessings. We will do everything in our hands to fulfill your desires."

Nell embraced her mother who began weeping out of both joy and sadness.

"What are your plans for the wedding?" Mr. Dumont asked.

"Father, a formal ceremony," Nell blissfully answered.

"A religious one? I mean, are you Catholic, Gabriel?"

"Yes, sir, I am," the young man responded rapidly. "Of course, we'll marry in a church."

"Thank God!" Mary sighed. And with that, the plans were set.

The following weeks were a difficult test for the Dumonts and Gabriel and Susan. To organize and take care of all the details a wedding demands occupied every second of the day. When the date of the marriage was agreed, Gabriel, using the new telegraph line, sent the news to his family. Previously, he had written a letter announcing his engagement. The Gilberts replied they were unable to travel north for the wedding due to distance and short time but they were eager to meet their daughter-in-law.

The wedding ceremony took place in a local church. Relatives and friends crowded the small chapel, confirming Nell's popularity. The bride, wearing an embroidered silk wedding dress; the tall, slim, bushy black hair groom, formed an elegant couple happily applauded. The Dumonts' mansion hosted the reception afterward. Susan, always at hand, made sure everything ran smoothly. Mary Dumont was too nervous; she could not handle such an event alone.

Francis, James Fitzgerald and other guests gathered in a room, away from the noisy, young people. When Gabriel happened to be near, Francis called him, "Come, have a drink with us." The groom walked into the room and took a glass of wine.

"So, you are from the South?" a gentleman addressed Gabriel.

"That is correct," he confirmed.

"I never traveled that far. I heard the country is beautiful. One of these days, I will go and see it myself," the gentleman promised.

"You will be welcomed," Gabriel assured.

"I'm really curious about your livelihood," the man said looking straight at him. "Particularly, the slaves."

"They are happy, treated well." Gabriel said turning his head to move on.

"Probably you read the Boston newspaper *The Liberator*," the guest continued, obligating the young man to face him again.

The subject seemed important to this person and no malice was in his voice as he went on. "More than one respectable citizen and legislator wants to eliminate slavery by gradual emancipation and colonization."

By now, everyone within close earshot had turned their attention to this conversation.

"To free the slaves would cause social chaos and racial catastrophe to the South. It is our way of life," Gabriel answered, repeating the arguments sustained by his fellowship concerning the controversial issue. "Besides, as you surely have heard, government has no authority over slavery."

"Please, no politics today," Francis said, coming between Gabriel and the inquiring gentleman. He took Gabriel by an arm and led him away a few steps, breaking the circle around the debating men. At that moment Susan came looking for Gabriel and Francis. She said the man had arrived with the new invention to take a photograph of the newlyweds with family and friends. Everybody followed Susan, Gabriel and Francis going out, joining Nell and Mary on the terrace. The man in charge of the new machine instructed everyone to form a group around the bride and groom, with the Dumonts, the Fitzgeralds and Susan at their side. Everyone put on their big smile, facing the man behind the marvelous machine and jumping a little when the bright light and noise indicated the photograph was taken.

Later, under the enthusiastic farewell of the Dumonts, Fitzgeralds, Susan and the rest of their friends, the happy couple went to the countryside to the mountains where their love first blossomed.

Francis, Mary, Susan and the Fitzgeralds gathered at the railroad station for the joyful and sad occasion of saying goodbye to the recently married couple. The time had come for them to go south. After an emotional exchange of kisses, embraces, and good wishes, the farewell party saw the locomotive pull the cars smoothly down the tracks, carrying Gabriel and Nell to their promising, happy new life and destiny.

Southerner

Nell and Gabriel enjoyed being free of pressures now that the business deal and the wedding were in the past. On the train ride to the South, they left the private compartment at dinnertime, greeting other passengers on their way to the dining car. The view outside changed; sporadic lights shining in the distance.

As the train continued, they left the cool North behind. Among the travelers entering the train, the ladies grew more reserved and even equally well dressed. Gabriel told Nell that soon they would be in the heart of the South.

The bright sunlight woke up Nell. She never had seen such lucid light so early. She stood and pulled the window curtain. A beautiful, awesome countryside view came to her eyes. Tall, green trees with big, round trunks, unlike the thin ones she knew covered all she could see. Their branches and leaves moved with the morning breeze, seeming to salute the passing train. And flowers, wildflowers everywhere, in a delightful symphony of colors.

"Gabriel, wake up!" She needed to show him this. He opened his eyes, wondering, *Why the commotion?*

"Come here! I have never seen anything like this!" Her enthusiastic voice gave him no alterative but to join her at the window.

"Oh, yes, I know this place. Better dress up. Soon we'll be at home."

Early midday, the train arrived at Roseville. As Gabriel and Nell stepped out, a couple of men approached them, one young and the other older. The young man embraced Gabriel with friendly, emotional impulse, the two greeting each other very warmly. The older man stood apart, watching. Nell looked at the pair of young men. In her circle, they did not act so effusively; anyway, she had expected to be greeted by someone from Gabriel's family.

"Nell, this is my good friend Dexter." Turning to her, Gabriel introduced the young man, who kissed her hand with a chivalrous gesture, making her blush. "More than a friend, he is my little brother," he continued, putting his arm around the man's shoulders. He turned to the older man. "Wade, take care of the luggage."

The man, followed by two black servants, went into the train. Gabriel, holding Nell's hand, his friend at the other side, walked through the station, greeting people coming in opposite direction; evidently, they were acquaintances. They reached a dusty, crowded street and approached a parked carriage.

"I need to tell you," his friend Dexter said as they reached the coach, "many things have happened lately." Gabriel helped Nell to get inside. The man called Wade and the servants came back carrying the luggage they put in the back of the vehicle. Gabriel and Dexter climbed in and sat facing Nell. Wade took control of the reins and with a scream he made the horses start trotting.

"Dexter, I saw Simon, your father's runaway slave in Boston," Gabriel said.

"Really?" the man was surprised.

The two friends constantly talked during the trip, exchanging news. Curiously, not a word was said about the wedding or bride. Nell, unfamiliar with rough roads, was continually shaken by the sudden movements as they rode over uneven terrain. She opted to pay more attention to the outside than to the two men, since they were too engrossed in their own conversation. She remembered Gabriel mentioning he had a close friend but it never crossed her mind that they would be so . . . intimate.

Soon the coach left town and entered a long stretch of road with land cultivated at both sides. Surely, Nell reasoned, these were plantations, the main agricultural occupation of these territories. The coach drove on for a time then diminished speed.

"Nell, dear, this is our estate." Gabriel, bending and taking her hands, indicated with a gesture of his head a tall, white fence now visible across the road. The coach made a turn, entering a long trail with tall trees at both sides. In some places, there were flowers and bushes, but it did not look as though the grounds had been taken care of recently. At the end of the road a big, two-story building. The coach stopped at the main entrance. A tall, strong-looking black woman came out of the house and opened the carriage door.

"Welcome home, Young Master Gabriel!" she greeted him, smiling.

Gabriel, followed by Dexter, came out, both helping Nell to step down. The black woman bowed at Nell. Nell was embarrassed, unaccustomed to such manners and not knowing how to reciprocate the salutation.

Gabriel put his arm around Nell's shoulders and guided her into the house, followed by Dexter and the black woman. They walked into a big, almost square room. An impeccably dressed and groomed man came in from a door near the entrance, approaching the group with an ample smile.

"Nell dear, Mr. Cecil Gilbert, my father."

"Gabriel, you have given me the most beautiful daughter-in-law!" the gentleman said, coming up to Nell and holding her hands with a friendly gesture.

"Thank you, Father. I knew you'd like her," Gabriel said, pleased with the warm reception. From a back door, two ladies came out, one walking faster than the other but slowing her steps before reaching the group to allow the second woman to get there first.

"Nell, this is my mother Edna," the newlywed made the introduction. Nell advanced to her and, holding hands, they smiled at each other.

"Welcome to our family, Nell," Gabriel's mother spoke in a soft but clear voice.

"And this is Aunt Mabel, our guardian angel," Gabriel added, signaling the second lady who coming to Nell, effusively embraced her.

"Dear, I am so glad to meet you! Finally, this nephew of mine has given me a new niece." Her voice was warm and amicable as she greeted the new addition to the family.

Nell, impressed at such lovely words directed to her, could only smile as she looked from one person to the other, unable to reply accordingly with similar phrases.

Gabriel's father, taking Nell by an arm, separated the close group. He said, "Dear, unfortunately my daughter Anne could not be here. She will come home from school soon."

"That is right! Gabriel told me he has a sister," Nell exclaimed, finally able to coordinate a thought and prove she had a voice and was capable of reasoning. She turned to everyone. "Thank you for this wonderful, hearty welcoming."

"You deserve this and much more," Gabriel's father responded.

"We have been expecting you and will help in anything you need," Aunt Mabel added.

"Thank you so much," Nell answered with genuine gratitude.

"Well, you surely are tired after the long trip. Gabriel, take your wife upstairs to your rooms and get some rest," Mr. Gilbert suggested. "We will see you again at dinner, as we are accustomed to."

Gabriel took Nell's hands and walked toward a staircase, which was not a typical one. Coming from the upper level, close to the wall, it ended slightly to the left, leaving more open space to the lower floor.

"Well, I'm leaving." Dexter said walking to the main entrance. "I'll see you soon."

Later, after a nap, Nell finished dressing as quickly as possible. She came out of the bedroom to a small but cozy parlor, where Gabriel was reading a newspaper. "Ready. Let's go."

"Nice, very elegant," Gabriel said, putting the paper down. "Come, sit down. My father likes punctuality but it is early; everybody is still in their rooms."

"Is your sister home?"

"Must be. She'll be there; nobody misses dinner. This is a family tradition strictly followed by my father."

"I expected to meet her after she came from school."

Gabriel said, "Probably she was advised not to disturb us."

"I see," Nell said. "So your aunt, is she your mother's sister?"

"No, she is the widow of my mother's brother."

"She is very friendly. I liked her instantly," Nell assured her husband.

"I'm glad. She is always ready to help. In the past I have followed her suggestions with very good results."

"Aunt and adviser . . . interesting." Although pretending seriousness, Nell could not avoid smiling; then, turning to laughter. Gabriel embraced her, amused by his wife's good humor.

When Gabriel and Nell came to the dining room, the Gilberts were already there, waiting for them.

"Do you feel better after resting, Nell?" Mr. Gilbert asked.

"Yes, it is so peaceful here."

"I am pleased you had a restful afternoon," Mr. Gilbert expressed, walking toward the table, followed by his wife and a young woman.

That must be Gabriel's sister. She's younger than I had imagined, Nell thought.

Gabriel and Nell sat opposite her new mother-in-law with Gilbert Senior at the head of the table. Curiously, Mrs. Edna Gilbert did not occupy the other end. Nell's eyes and the girl met. She could no longer wait.

"Are you Anne?" Nell asked as she sat down across from her. She answered with a 'yes' gesture of the head, her eyes moving down to the table cloth.

"I forgot Anne did not meet you," Mr. Gilbert admitted. "My apologies, Nell. We are so excited with your presence that my mind is not working properly."

"Please, Mr. Gilbert. I am a little out of my senses too. Afraid to make a mistake, give you a wrong impression."

"Not at all, Nell. I am sure my son made the right election. Anne, kiss your sister-in-law."

The girl, a petit light hair youngster, stood up, went around the table, and embraced Nell.

"Anne, I am very glad to meet you. Gabriel talked to me about you," Nell said, trying to break the girl's shyness. Smiling, Anne returned rapidly to her seat under her parents' watchful eyes.

The black woman who had welcomed Nell came into the room carrying a tray with roasted turkey. She put it close to Mrs. Gilbert and then stood behind her.

"Nell, this is LaBelle. If there's anything you need, ask her," Gabriel's mother introduced her. She took a fork and a knife and started cutting the roasted bird. The black woman almost smiled looking at Nell but she rapidly lowered her eyes to the ground. Two young black women came with food dishes; one was put near Mr. Gilbert, the other close to Gabriel and his wife. Both women left as quickly and silently as they had entered.

After dinner the Gilberts went into an adjacent room at the center of which was a plush couch where Mrs. Gilbert sat, Anne at her side. Nell, after some hesitation, sat on a sofa opposite the two ladies. Gabriel and his father remained standing by a glass wall near the end of the parlor.

The black woman, LaBelle, came forward followed by two servants carrying trays with fruits, sweets, and tea. They displayed the refreshments on a coffee table nearby. LaBelle asked "Miss Nell" what she wanted. Due more to the situation than desire, she declined anything. Anyway, she had had an abundant meal, leaving no appetite for anything else. LaBelle served tea to Mrs. Gilbert and Anne had sweets. The two younger servants left while LaBelle stood near the entrance, quiet and alert.

Mr. Gilbert started lighting a cigar. Realizing he was in the company of someone whose opinion about smoking he did not know, he quickly turned to Nell and asked, "Do you mind?"

"Not at all," she replied. In reality, smoke annoyed her but being new in their company, she did not want to appear problematic. Mr. Gilbert accepted her approval with a hand gesture and finished lighting the cigar. Soon, a strong smell and tobacco smoke filled the place.

"Gabriel, to introduce your wife to our friends, we must organize a presentation ball," Mr. Gilbert said.

Nell looked at the two men. Gabriel agreed with his father, who continued, "Go to Charleston or other city and hire a good orchestra. Nell will come down the stairs . . . "

"Oh, no!" Nell jumped into the conversation. "I cannot do that."

Gabriel came closer to her. He knew she was not familiar with their customs; such display in the presentation ball was normal for them, but new for his wife.

"Nell, don't worry. This is done by every young woman. Though, if you disagree my father will understand," Gabriel anticipated.

Nell stood; holding hands with Gabriel so she'd feel more secure. She was too down to earth; just could not show herself off in this arrogant, in her opinion display, no matter how common such an introduction was considered in the South. "I'm sorry. I do not want to spoil your plans, but I simply cannot do it." Nell said shaken a little, looking straight at her father-in-law.

"There is nothing to be afraid of," Mr. Gilbert responded, approaching from the back of the room and stopping close to his son and daughter-in-law. "We will be there. Our friends will be delighted to meet you."

Mrs. Gilbert put her cup of tea on the tray. Anne, at her mother's side, quietly followed the exchange of words.

"It is not my upbringing," Nell explained firmly, now more relaxed.

"We understand and agree with that," Gabriel quickly said, siding with her and trying to arrange conditions for a compromise. "Nobody will ask you to do something you do not want," he finished, looking at his father.

But the head of the family took control. "This is how we present young women, new members into our society. Of course, each community does it according to whatever tradition they are accustomed to." Mr. Gilbert explained in a low tone as he paced up and down, filling the salon with smoke. He hoped his words would bring understanding to this young woman, already married to his son, yet acting so out of place.

"Father," Gabriel said, "she is not aware of our customs. She just moved here."

Slowly, the gentleman of the mansion walked toward the center of the room. LaBelle went to the coffee table, picked up the tray with the tea service, and left the room.

"Well, you must explain to your wife our manners. Of course, she needs not to follow them, but will be difficult for our friends to understand it if she doesn't." Mr. Gilbert answered calmly, pacing back to the end of the parlor.

"Mr. Gilbert," Nell said, facing her father-in-law, "I don't mean to reject the custom. I now live in the South and I'm willing to follow your ways. But it's too soon to completely change my personality. Surely, this is a joyful tradition but I am not ready yet."

Silence and heavy smoke from the cigar filled the room. Gabriel looked at his father; he knew that Mr. Gilbert Senior kept his views and very few had the nerves to disagree with him. On the contrary, many of his associates frequently asked for his advice.

Mother and daughter glanced at each other silently as Mr. Gilbert came to the center of the room, puffing his cigar and looking at Gabriel and Nell.

"Well, how do you suggest to be presented?" Mr. Gilbert asked, surprising his family by not insisting on their tradition, a very rare attitude.

"Gabriel will escort me," Nell said, hoping her solution would be agreeable to all.

"If this is what you want, that is how it shall be," Cecil Gilbert accepted, ending the growing tension.

The subject was not discussed again. That amazed the house members. Probably, they guessed, Mr. Gilbert was simply allowing someone else's opinion to prevail as a gentleman's courtesy, honoring from whom it came. Anyway, it was too early to disagree with his new daughter-in-law.

The Gilbert mansion was transformed for the presentation ball. Nell could not believe the time was already here. The numerous details to handle had made the days leading up to the ball too short. Thank God LaBelle was the perfect assistant. No matter what task she was assigned, she did it. Even when the dress Nell was to wear that night needed few alterations, LaBelle handled it as an experienced seamstress. Nell was impressed with the abilities, the problem-solving capabilities that this woman had. LaBelle was not only loyal but competent.

At sunset, carriages started to appear in the wide entrance trail. Slave men better dressed than normally directed the traffic once the guests reached the main entrance. Soon the ceremonial hall was crowded. Everyone invited had honored the request. Cecil and Edna Gilbert received them with the customary Southern courtesy.

Nell, escorted by Gabriel, descended the semicircular staircase. Fortunately for Nell's nerves, the orchestra filled the silence left by the audience curiously watching the couple coming down. All eyes were on the white skin, blonde hair, and big blue eyes of the young woman graciously entering their unique, respectable world. Instantly, everyone agreed that they were in the presence of someone different, yet worthy of being accepted into their society not just because she was a Gilbert but on her personal merits.

The newlyweds stood in the center of the hall. Cecil, Edna and Anne joined them. The procession immediately began. Gabriel's father announced the guests' names as they shook hands and embraced the smiling couple. Nell found it a great task to memorize so many faces with their respective surnames. After a while, she gave up; it was impossible. Therefore, she concentrated on smiling and reciprocating salutations as the guests came on. Gabriel would just have to refresh her memory since the number of neighbors, close friends, and associates seemed to have no end. However, a few faces were familiar: Dexter and his parents and Aunt Mabel, who was happy and excited about the gala.

When the last couple passed, Nell and Gabriel sat. Still, some came back to reaffirm their best wishes. Several servants came out, offering drinks and delicacies. Many couples, following the merry notes of the orchestra, went to the center of the room to dance. Nell and Gabriel joined them, the others opening space to the happy couple. Everyone was enjoying the festival celebration and admiring Nell the young ladies, called Belles in this territory had mastered the rules of etiquette and the dances, waltzing to and fro and fluttering their fans with such elegance. It was a priceless, memorable night. To Nell's eyes, it was also a confirmation of the level of friendship and prestige the name *Gilbert* had in this community, reaffirming the high opinion of her new family.

Gabriel had promised to take Nell on a tour of the plantation, which she had not yet seen. Near the mansion's main entrance, Wade was holding the horse attached to a buggy by its harness. The couple got into the carriage. Wade stepped aside, releasing the animal. Gabriel took control of the reins and put the vehicle in motion, going down the road.

Once they were a short distance away, Nell said, "I don't like that man."

"Wade? He is efficient. My father does not say that about many of his employees."

"Whenever he is around, I don't feel comfortable."

"He will not do anything knowing we disapprove of it," Gabriel explained. "Maybe he is not the most likeable man, but he's always ready to do whatever we order."

A few yards farther, Gabriel turned the carriage out onto a narrow trail. Both sides were lined by tall, thick trees, whose branches seemed to dance with the brisk wind. The breeze refreshed the face, making Nell feel as if she was floating in the air, flying as the surrounding butterflies were, going from one flower to another.

"This is amazing . . . is paradise!" Nell exclaimed, standing on the buggy and admiring the astonishing, colorful view all around. The surroundings were so peaceful, yet full of sound. Gabriel smiled. This scenery was familiar for him; he had seen it so often that his eyes were more than accustomed to it. Anyway, he looked at it again, trying to rediscover the splendid forest, feel the enchanting, unique wonder that had caused in Nell that explosive burst of enthusiasm, happiness . . . which gradually fell behind as the horse carried the buggy down the trail into a plainer, cultivated terrain.

"This is our cotton plantation," Gabriel informed, pointing to both sides.

The harvest appeared with its indisputable features. For the first time Nell saw the raw material, cotton, so widely used, though she'd never seen it in its origins. Gabriel pulled on the bridle a little, slowing the carriage and allowing his wife to admire the white fluff amid the bushes so compact, but separated from each other. Suddenly she saw the slaves everywhere, picking up cotton balls. They seemed to notice the presence of the visitors but did not raise their heads, keeping diligently at work. Nell saw children, young boys and girls just as busy and dedicated as their elders. As she looked at them, some rare feelings ran through her. Momentarily, she turned her gaze away from the fields. Then, gradually, singing was coming from the plantation.

"They are welcoming you, love," Gabriel explained, hearing the voices louder and louder, a profound, grave tone coming from every part.

"What are they saying?" Nell asked.

"I do not know," Gabriel answered. "Nobody comprehends them."

He guided the vehicle away, back to the main road. Still the sound reached their ears, part gospel, wild but unmistakably religious, reverent, holy.

That night at dinner Nell was quiet.

"Enjoy the visit to the country, Nell?" Mr. Gilbert asked.

"It was interesting," she replied. "I've never seen such beautiful forest. That's how I imagine 'paradise' is. But the people, depressing."

"They sang for Nell, Father," Gabriel said quickly, trying to dissipate the sadness in his wife's voice.

Cecil Gilbert put a bite into his mouth, swallowed it and cleaned his lips with a napkin. "Depressing?"

Anne looked at Nell. She knew her father never let anything without a proper explanation. Quickly the young girl lowered her eyes and continued eating.

"Nell is not familiar with slavery," Gabriel said in Nell's defense.

"I realize it is the system," Nell said. "No doubt. But they are in so deplorable conditions . . . and the children; it gives me cold chills all over my body."

Silence fell, interrupted only by the noise of forks and spoons hitting the dinnerware. LaBelle moved nervously behind the masters.

"This is their natural state. They are happy, better off enslaved," Mr. Gilbert solemnly declared, his tone firm as he repeated the great, commonly Southerner truth.

"Would you be happy if you were a slave?" Nell's question came out spontaneously, before she realized its impertinence. Mr. Gilbert, stunned, dropped his hand and fork to the table and looked at his daughter-in-law, his eyes turning red and his face contracting. How she dared to think *he* could be a slave? Was she insane? He could hardly keep control and did not explode in righteous anger. LaBelle hurriedly took empty dishes and left the room.

"Nell, you have a strange mind!" Cecil Gilbert answered with cold voice, soft words, though stronger one he would have used in other circumstances. The rest of the dinner followed quietly.

Routine was coming back to Gabriel as he and Nell settled in. He explained to his wife that he had neglected obligations and left his father alone with the supervision of the business. It was about time he assumed his part of responsibilities that he'd put aside to get Nell familiar with her new household. Therefore, now she would be alone and have time to arrange the apartment as she pleased. From the small parlor entering her rooms, though, she could see Gabriel in his father's office if somebody leaves the door open, as frequently happened.

Nell was fixing the bedspread when a knock at the door stopped her. It was LaBelle who came in with a young slave-servant.

"Miss Nell, I told already; you don't need to do this. It is the job of this girl."

"Mrs. Nell," she corrected LaBelle, who was already busy at one side of the bed, the helper at the other, covering it with an ornamental blanket. Nell sat close to the window overlooking the main entrance and Cecil's office. She observed the fast, precise movements of both women. The efficiency was because of LaBelle's directing. Nell marveled at how whatever she did, she did it right. Surely, Edna Gilbert's trust in her was justified. Moments later, LaBelle asked Nell if there was anything else she wanted. Nell stood up and went toward the two women.

"No, LaBelle, thank you. What is your name?" she asked kindly, looking at the helper, who was half hidden behind LaBelle. The girl had not said a word.

"Miss Nell, you do not thank us. If you need anything, call me," the loyal LaBelle said rapidly, diverting Nell's question. Turning her back, she walked to the exit, pushing out the shy helper first and closing the door after her.

Nell smiled. Still unfamiliar with how to treat slaves, she wanted to find a way to do it but without the rigorous rules, as far as she knew, used in every mansion in the South. But then noisy steps coming from downstairs broke her thoughts. She went to the window and, separating the curtains, she saw Dexter going inside Cecil's office. She did not know he had business with her father-in-law.

Moments later she saw Gabriel and Dexter coming out of the office, walking a few steps into the hall. Dexter was excited, talking fast and gesticulating; Gabriel looked serious, paying close attention to Dexter's explanations. Gabriel talked to him with unfriendly gesture. They were evidently arguing over the subject. Nell observed both men going back and forth, Dexter constantly expressing his arguments which seemed not to please to other party. Finally, they went back into Cecil's office.

Later that evening, Gabriel entered the parlor of his apartment smiling. "Nell, love, where's my queen?" A happy Nell came out from the connecting bedroom, embraced and kissed him.

"I don't want to be noisy," she said, separating from him, "but I could not avoid seeing you and Dexter downstairs. Is there a problem?"

"Ah, you saw us," Gabriel replied walking apart. Nell noticed the matter was unpleasant for him. She kept quiet, allowing him to decide whether if to talk about it.

"He is in trouble." Gabriel finally said, putting hands into his trousers' pockets, sorrow in his voice. "An abolitionist was hanged not long ago. Dexter is accused of participating in it."

"Sorry to hear that."

"These things did not happen for a long time," Gabriel said, visibly annoyed. He explained, pacing, "Agitators, lunatics are coming. People are tired of them. This lynching is not right; it's obviously against the law but there's nothing we can do and it will happen again if they continue coming with their crazy ideas of emancipation."

Although these lines of thinking were questionable to Nell, she opted not to disagree with Gabriel who sided with the community that he was a part of.

"I want to help him, but how?" Gabriel continued, visibly unhappy.

Why does this affect him so much? Nell wondered, but at the same time she wished to find some way to ease her husband's dismay. "Ask Dexter what you can do."

"My father is in contact with his lawyers; trying to find a way out." Saying this, Gabriel changed his mood. Smiling, he embraced his wife. "Aunt Mabel is coming tomorrow to go shopping, remember?"

"Of course. Roseville is one of the places I have not visited yet."

"It is not a big town. I hope it won't disappoint you."

"Of course, not. Anyway, I like small villages."

The next morning, Nell dressed as fast as possible and went downstairs. She wanted to see Gabriel at work with his father, but before she reached the lower floor, Aunt Mabel came in through the main entrance.

"Good morning, Nell, dear," she saluted with friendly voice as her niece-in-law stepped off the last stair. "Are ready to go?"

"Yes, I am."

"Just let me say hello to Edna first."

Nell knew her mother-in-law had separated chambers below, but so far she'd had no opportunity to visit her; it was one of those things that took time for a newcomer to get acquainted with. She followed Aunt Mabel, who knocked on the door. Moments later it was opened by Edna Gilbert. The woman's face, downcast a second before, seemed to change at the sight of Nell. Almost smiling, Edna invited her visitors to come inside.

"We're just here for a moment, Edna. Nell and I are going to Roseville. This girl has not been in town," Aunt Mabel explained walking into the room with Nell after her. Nell examined the place. It was neat, soberly furnished, and elegant, generally old-fashioned. They sat on an overstuffed couch. Aunt Mabel and Edna started talking. Nell observed them as the two different women exchanged small talk of trivial, daily activities in a cordial, warm way. When it was time to leave, both women embraced.

"Come with us to Roseville," Nell suddenly proposed to Edna but the older woman rejected the notion.

"You need to go out," Nell insisted.

"I certainly do not. Obviously, it is not my desire to go," Edna said slowly in her habitual, low tone, disappointing Nell. She wanted to win her confidence, get closer to her. Aunt Mabel took Nell by an arm, saying good-bye and leaving the room.

"Nell, dear, Edna is very conservative; for a long, long time she has not visited town."

"I just wanted to be friendly."

"My dear, I know; you have plenty of time for that," Aunt Mabel reminded the girl, trying to eliminate, at least in part Nell's frustration with the incident.

They stopped at Cecil's office. Aunt Mabel knocked and opened the door. They walked into an elegant office; on one side a wooden cabinet with rifles and guns.

"Good morning, gentlemen!" Aunt Mabel trumpeted, advancing to Mr. Gilbert sitting on an expensive armchair; Gabriel standing at his side. "How are you, Cecil?"

Gabriel came to Nell.

"I am well, Aunt Mabel," the head of the family said, standing up. "I need not ask you; always so vibrant and young."

"Not true. You are the one better and better."

"Because you look at me with friendly eyes," Cecil answered gallantly. "Going to town, I believe?" He said with a more serious tone, gazing at Nell.

"Yes. We will visit all the dressmakers in Roseville," Aunt Mabel jovially asserted.

"Before you go, Nell, I have a present for you," Cecil announced, exiting the room under the surprised looks of the ladies. Nell turned to Gabriel, asking with her eyes. He pointed back to the door. Cecil Gilbert came back, followed by the servant slave LaBelle and a younger black girl.

"Nell, she is for you," Cecil informed his daughter-in-law, gesturing at the girl as he went back to the executive chair.

Nell was amazed, uncomprehending.

"She will be at your service," Gabriel explained holding Nell's hands.

This was so unthinkable that it left her speechless.

"Your name is?" Gabriel asked the girl.

"Clydette," she answered with chilly voice, shy smile.

"How old?" Cecil questioned.

"Twelve."

"Ten!" LaBelle rectified her, stepping closer, holding the girl by an arm.

"Well, Nell?" Master Gilbert asked, waiting for the corresponding gratitude.

Nell simply said, "I do not know."

"Having someone at your service is appropriate," Gabriel said, coming to the rescue. "In a few days you will see how helpful she is."

"I need no help," Nell stated. She was thinking, *She is too young.*

"Yes, you do," Cecil corrected her.

"Of course, dear," Aunt Mabel joined, completing the circle trying to overcome the reluctance of the new Southerner. "She will be a great aide."

"No doubt. This girl will be at Nell's service," Mr. Gilbert ceremoniously declared from his high chair.

The little young woman seemed so defenseless, although she kept a serene attitude, shy smile and had a sense of conformity. And since nobody ventured to disagree with Mr. Gilbert's proclamation, Nell broke her hesitation. Case closed; she now had a personal servant.

"Nell, a word of advice," Mr. Gilbert added, "see that she always washes her hands."

With that, Aunt Mabel turned to go. "Nell, dear, it's time to leave."

Gabriel stepped in. "I cannot go now," he said. "Wade will drive you there. I'll pick you up later. And don't forget, Anne will join you after school."

Nell was surprised. Her husband was supposed to accompany them. However, he explained that certain business required his presence there.

"The girl will go," Cecil decided. "It'll be a good opportunity to get to know her." The ladies accepted; Nell felt she couldn't refuse. With that, they left the office, escorted by Gabriel to the main entrance, LaBelle instructing the new slave girl. Outside, a carriage under Wade's control waited.

Roseville was indeed small. But nothing was missing as Nell noticed all kinds of stores, including various dressmakers with a splendid variety of fabrics, silk in great supply. Some owners were extremely interested in selling their wares, hawking them on the walkways. The passersby were all friendly people, though some of them noisy, as Nell noticed. Aunt Mabel explained that as 'natural curiosity'. Nell was a new face in town. Clydette walked a few steps ahead as Aunt Mabel directed her.

"Oh, oh! She is a close friend of your in-laws!" Aunt Mabel warned Nell as she spotted a young, elegantly dressed woman ahead. Nell instantly remembered her. She was the only one at the presentation ball who had effusively embraced and congratulated Gabriel first; everybody else had greeted Nell since she was standing ahead.

"Aunt Mabel, Mrs. Gilbert, what a surprise!" she called merrily approaching the couple with friendly gesture. She embraced Aunt Mabel and shook hands with Nell.

"Shopping, Darlene?"

"Not I, Aunt Mabel. Mother is at one of these stores. I could not bear the heat, so I came out to take fresh air," she replied, talking fast and smiling as her eyes shifted back and forth between Aunt Mabel and Nell. "Mrs. Gilbert, do you like our town?"

Nell answered, "This is my first visit; I haven't had time yet to see much."

"Ah, here is Anne," Aunt Mabel said, pointing straight. Nell and Darlene turned their heads. Soon, Anne appeared and joined them.

"Anne, dear!" Advancing, opening wide her arms, Darlene embraced the girl, who evidently did not expect such a warm greeting.

"Hello, Darlene," the youngster responded. Coming closer, she greeted Aunt Mabel and Nell.

"Better keep walking," Aunt Mabel suggested. "We have not visited important stores. Time is running out. Say hello to your mother, Darlene," she added, turning back to the family friend.

"I will, I will," Darlene answered, her eyes following the group as they walked away, unaware that she may had expected to be invited to join their shopping day.

Smiling, the Gilberts women continued, checking store after store.

"Is she with us?" Anne asked curiously, noticing the young black girl ahead.

"Yes, she is at my service," Nell informed Anne, "a courtesy from my father-in-law."

"Right. LaBelle mentioned she would bring a relative," Anne said, gazing at the young slave who, always smiling, was jumping around to avoid oncoming people.

Across the dusty street, Nell saw a big sign reading "Negroes Sold," which gave her a cold chill. Lowering her eyes, she kept up a rapid pace to leave it behind, still unfamiliar with the institution and the realities of this land.

"Nell, this is the best dressmaker in town," Aunt Mabel announced as she turned to the entrance of a store. She opened the door, allowing the other three women to enter first.

"Ladies, welcome to my humble boutique!" Smiling, a middle-aged man came from behind a long counter, saluted with a foreign *faked* accent, according to Nell, the approaching incoming clients.

"Good afternoon, Monsieur Pierre."

"Madam, a great pleasure to see you. How can I help? We have just received new materials, and if you like silk, here can find the best."

"Monsieur Pierre, let me introduce you my nephew Gabriel's wife, the new Mrs. Gilbert," Aunt Mabel, turning to Nell, made the presentation. "I am sure you heard about her already."

"It is a great honor to meet and welcome Mrs. Gilbert," the proprietor said with reverence. "My employees and I are at your orders."

"Monsieur Pierre, I need gloves," Aunt Mabel said, walking toward the counter, followed by Anne and Nell.

The store owner rapidly went to the other side of the counter. With a hand gesture he called for a female clerk who was standing not far away. She diligently removed a box from the shelf and put it on the counter. M. Pierre opened it, took out various pairs of gloves and set them on display.

"These are made with very delicate fabric, as you can see," he ceremoniously described to the attentive ladies. Anne, separating from them, perused the articles on display, stopping to look at hats. A young boy arranging boxes not far discreetly looked at her.

"Please, can you help me?" Anne requested.

The employee immediately came.

"I would like to see that hat, the one at the top," Anne solicited. The young man went to the end of the room, picked up a ladder, and came back. He put it on the wall and climbed to retrieve the item requested. Anne took the hat and reviewed it.

"You go to Roseville's Ladies Academy," the clerk said smiling.

"How you know?"

"I delivered merchandise there last week. I saw you."

Just then Aunt Mabel called, "Anne, where are you?"

"Down there," Nell said, signaling the counter down.

"Did you find something?" Aunt Mabel questioned coming to her.

"Is it not lovely?" Anne moved the hat in her hands, showing it.

The owner had followed the ladies. "Anson, made a sale? Good! You are advancing very well," he congratulated the youngster, who was as surprised as Anne at the announcement. Nell and Aunt Mabel admired the hat. Since everybody approved it and Anne, not wanting to embarrass the employee, accepted it. The sale, considered realized.

"Mrs. Gilbert, anything you like?" M. Pierre asked, trying to be of service to everyone.

"I need nothing today; maybe next time," Nell answered politely.

Turning around she saw Clydette standing at the entrance. Her dress was a mess.

"Mr. Pierre, do you have something for her?" she asked, not knowing how out of place the request was.

The shop owner ignored her, keeping busy placing the hat inside a big box. He called his employee to wrap it, thinking, *is this lady out of her mind? My boutique, selling dresses to slaves?* His thoughts showed on his face.

Nell noticed the adverse reaction, but she was disappointed. *For goodness sake*, she thought, *it's for a little girl. How hurtful it could be?*

"Time to leave. Ready, Anne?" Aunt Mabel declared.

"Anson, carry the hatbox and gloves to the ladies' carriage," M. Pierre ordered.

"We can do it," Nell informed the owner.

"Not at all, Madame. He is here to serve you," Giving the boy the packages, the owner left no doubt the way things are handled in his shop. Therefore, Nell accepted the offer. *Another custom to assimilate*, she said to herself.

"Ladies, it has been a pleasure to serve you, and especially to meet Mrs. Gilbert."

"Good-by, Monsieur Pierre," Aunt Mabel said walking through the door that was being held open by the smiling proprietor to reinforce his gratefulness.

Back on the dusty street, they walked straight, Anne, Anson, and Clydette first. Aunt Mabel pointed out things of interest, such as the meeting house, where people gathered to discuss problems and other relevant subjects.

They approached the next boutique. "Here is another dressmaker. She is not as fancy as M. Pierre, but if you want, we can stop by," Aunt Mabel suggested.

"Maybe other day; it is getting late. Where is Gabriel supposed to meet us?" Nell questioned.

"Don't worry, he'll find us. No place to hide here," Aunt Mabel answered in her usual, merry tone.

But Nell was getting impatient. She looked around wishing to see him. Across the street, an old well-dressed woman was staring at them without restraint.

"Let us go inside this store," Aunt Mabel said stopping suddenly at an entrance. She waited for the youngsters and Nell to get in but Anson; then she followed. Soon, a middle-aged man approached the group, offering his assistance. Aunt Mabel acknowledged him. Walking around, she checked different pieces of fabric on display; the salesperson solicitously describing the merchandise.

After a while, she thanked the man and came back to the entrance, where Nell, Anne, and Clydette waited. They went out. The sun was less brilliant, the street not as crowded; night was falling. Soon, the shopping ladies saw a carriage coming down the street driven by Wade. He stopped close, helped them to get inside and explained Gabriel had been unable to come. Anson gave to Wade the big box, which he secured in the back. Taking the reins, Wade directed the coach down the road under a big sign announcing a coming county fair.

"Wade, I am not going back to Gilbert's mansion. Drop me off at my house," Aunt Mabel requested.

"Certainly, Madam."

The ride was uneventful, and soon everyone was home. Nell and Anne walked into the large entrance of the mansion, followed by Wade, carrying the big box, and Clydette, last. Nell saw Gabriel in Cecil's office; the door was half-open. She heard voices; evidently, a meeting was on. That was rare. Since she was living there, her father-in-law never had company so late.

Afterward, when Gabriel came up he told Nell the town judge had questioned him about Dexter. That was why he could not go to Roseville. He wanted to help his friend but there was little he could do because he was in Boston when the lynching of the abolitionist happened. The only favorable thing he could say is that Dexter knows where the keys of the Gilberts' country cottage are hidden; therefore, this corroborated his claim that he had been staying there after going hunting the night the hanging happened.

This matter really worried Nell. "Gabriel, please. I understand you want to assist your friend, but be careful."

"Don't worry, love. I will," he assured.

"I hope so," she answered. "Now hurry up and get ready or we will be late for dinner."

"Yes, Father does not like to wait." Hurriedly, he started undressing.

Nell mentioned, "A Country Fair is coming soon. Can we go?"

"Of course; we never miss such gatherings. We do not have much amusement around here, so we can't afford to ignore chances like that," Gabriel said, entering the bathroom.

The County Fair turned out to be big, with all kinds of exhibits and attractions. As Nell strolled through the never-ending countryside with Gabriel, Anne, and her permanent companion, Clydette wearing a new dress, she again noticed the great popularity her new family enjoyed. They did not walk far without answering salutations from people. Later, Gabriel left to take care of some business but he promised to come back to bring them home. The three women continued admiring the different amenities. The sun was bright but not too hot, as a fresh breeze helped them to go on.

"Good afternoon!"

The loud, unexpected salutation came from behind, causing Nell and company to stop. Turning, they saw Darlene, the family's close friend.

"How are you, Anne?" Darlene said, embracing the youngster. Anne was not amused by the overly zealous greeting.

"Mrs. Gilbert, we meet again," Darlene said facing Nell.

"Yes, what a surprise," she answered trying to be amiable. But without any apparent reason, her presence gave Nell an unpleasant feeling.

"Are you alone? Where are the Gilberts?" Darlene asked, gazing around.

"Gabriel will come soon," Nell informed the curious woman.

"I see. And your parents, Anne?"

"They are fine," the young lady responded, looking around. Silence followed. It seemed they had nothing to share in common.

"Well . . . I guess I'll join my parents," Darlene decided. "They're probably where the band is. My father loves music." She paused; apparently waiting for a response, then flashed a smile and walked away waving a hand.

Nell, Anne, and Clydette continued ahead. *Thank God Darlene left*, Nell thought. They kept looking at the exhibits, different attractions, some with noisy attendants. Nell spotted the young man who was employed at M. Pierre's boutique standing in a tent but she said nothing. He saw them as well when they crossed in front of him. He started following and reached them.

"Hello!" the young boy called as he stepped ahead.

"Good afternoon, young man," Nell responded, continuing walking. No one seemed interested talking with him.

"Did you see the horses?" the boy questioned Anne, walking at her side.

"No, not yet," Anne responded calmly. Secretly she was thinking, *Horses? Who cares?* Her facial expression remained dull.

"They have Arab racing horses," the boy continued, showing great enthusiasm for the subject, "Thoroughbreds and Palominos."

"Well, you seem very fond of those animals," Nell noted.

"Madam, I grew up with horses," he admitted. "My father was in charge of a horse farm years ago in Kentucky."

"That explains it," Nell observed.

Anne asked, "You live with your parents?"

"With my father; my mother passed away."

"I'm sorry," Anne condoled him.

"It happened a long time ago. My father and I get along very well," the young boy added, smiling to shake off the sadness of the previous news.

"How long have you worked for Mr. Pierre?" Nell asked changing to a more pleasant topic.

"Not long, but I want to learn another occupation."

Nell advised, "Well, you are young and can do whatever you want."

The coming and going of people watching the exhibits along the way made the walking amusing but tiresome.

"Hey, do you like ice cream?" the boy asked Anne.

Her eyes lit up. "Yes. Do they have any here?"

"I saw a place down this way. I'll tell you when we reach it."

"And your name was?" Nell interrupted the couple, not that she disapproved of their conversation but she just wanted to get things straight.

"Anson," Anne answered facing her sister-in-law.

"That's right," Nell said recalling it.

"I am glad you remember," Anson told Anne looking at her, his face radiant.

They continued walking, browsing the exhibits, sharing pleasant moments and developing friendship. A pavilion caught Anne's attention. Since Nell was not interested, she let her and Anson go, noting that Anne's formerly unenthusiastic mood toward the boy had warmed somewhat. She kept walking down the path, holding Clydette at her side; the place was too crowded and Anne and Anson were old enough to take care of themselves.

Nell returned the salutations of passersby, surely friends of Gabriel as they walked. She occasionally turned her head to check on Anne and Anson, who were now at a fountain getting refreshments. She continued walking. Many of the products presented did not get her attention; this was another world, not the one she knew and missed.

Later, Gabriel and his father joined Nell. They noticed Anne's absence. Nell explained she was with a friend, increasing the suspicion in her father-in-law's eyes when they heard Anne was with somebody the two men didn't know.

"Clydette, go," Nell instructed her. "Tell Anne we are waiting."

"Where?"

"That sign that says 'Refreshments.' See it?"

"I not know, Miss," Clydette responded.

"See the big letters?" Nell asked her, pointing to the sign.

"Yeah," the servant answered, smiling.

"What does it say, Clydette?" Nell insisted.

"I not know, Miss Nell," she said timidly.

"Oh, my God." The new Southerner suddenly realized her aide's limitations. "Go there and tell Anne to come back quickly," she said, pushing the girl away. "Clydette cannot read," she realized. Then she promised, "I will teach her."

"That is not necessary," the elder Gilbert said, waving her off.

A group of young men, talking loudly, came passing by. Dexter was among them. When he saw Gabriel and family, rapidly he approached them.

"Gabriel!" the young man shouted. "Mr. Cecil Gilbert and Mrs. Gilbert, glad to see you all!"

"Hello, men." Gabriel, raising an arm, greeted the group accompanying his friend, who was moving erratically. "How are you?" he said, smiling as he put an arm around Dexter's shoulders.

"Very well as you can see."

Gabriel stepped away with his friend. "Dexter, what are you doing?"

"Having a good time, my brother," the man responded, bobbing his head. "You know, Mrs. Gilbert is very elegant. When I get married, my wife and yours will be very good friends. We'll go everywhere together."

"Yes, *if* you behave well."

"I did not tell you yet. Come and let me say it to your father, too," Dexter said, pulling Gabriel back to Nell and Cecil. "Mr. Gilbert, Judge Davis dropped all charges against me."

"That is great news!" Gabriel said.

"You see? I have good reasons to celebrate," Dexter added, embracing Gabriel. Not far away, Dexter's friends applauded.

"Congratulations," Mr. Gilbert said, shaking hands with the young man.

The notice relieved Nell. She also joined expressing her joy to Dexter, who again explained the judge's decision: "Lack of evidence. Yeah, the case is closed."

Gabriel advised his friend to be more prudent. Shortly afterward, Dexter left with his friends. Cecil Gilbert breathed, relaxed. He was not comfortable around youngsters. Besides, right now he had more important matters to attend.

"Ah, here she comes," Nell announced. Anne, Anson, and Clydette approached, but before reaching them, Anson separated and disappeared into the crowd.

"Where have you been?" Cecil asked Anne. "You should be with your sister-in-law."

"I went for ice cream at that exhibit over there," Anne answered.

"Who is that boy?" Her father continued questioning.

"His name is Anson," Nell promptly answered, taking Anne by an arm. She started walking, putting the group in motion and distracting from the interrogatory. "He works at Mr. Pierre's boutique." Nell's information calmed the inquiring.

A few steps farther, Mr. Gilbert made a comment about Clydette's dress. Nell explained that LaBelle made it of "discarded" garments (which was not completely true) but she figured this way her in-law could not argue much. Nell explained since Clydette was always to accompany her, she needed to be properly dressed. Gabriel agreed.

Late that night, Nell and Gabriel already sleeping they were awakened by stones hitting the window and yelling. Gabriel separated the curtains seeing Dexter and friends outside, in the entrance trail on horses. He opened the window.

"Gabriel, going hunting. Come!" Dexter shouted.

"At this hour? Are you crazy?" Gabriel yelled back.

This time he didn't accept his invitation as not long ago he used to. Dexter insisted but the denials from upstairs were firm. The young man signaled his friends and screaming, they directed their mounts to the way out of the grounds.

"Miss Nell, a letter." LaBelle, entering the room with other servant, handed her an envelope.

"Thanks."

"Miss Nell, you don't thank me," the housekeeper reminded her.

"I know, but I do it automatically, as you call me 'miss' not 'missus'."

LaBelle, shaking her head, started to arrange the bed with the help of the other woman. She asked if Clydette, who was standing close to Nell, could help, because, "to be good to her Master, she must learn."

Nell agreed to let the girl help them.

"Miss Darlene is downstairs, talking to Master Mrs. Gilbert," LaBelle said without stopping working, gazing over her shoulder at Nell, reading the letter.

"Is she a frequent visitor?"

"Oh, yes! She used to come every day when she was Young Gabriel's . . . " LaBelle stopped abruptly, realizing she may have said something inappropriate. Quickly, changing her attention to Clydette, she instructed her how to fold the bedspread. Nell noticed the slip but did not say anything so as not to make the loyal slave feel uncomfortable. Besides, her instincts suggested that she must not appear worried at all.

"Miss Nell," LaBelle said, preparing to leave with the other woman, "Clydette will be outside the door during the night if need anything."

"That is not necessary," Nell replied.

"Master Gilbert told me."

"I will not need her late at night."

"Miss Nell, we do what he says," LaBelle insisted, visibly disturbed. How could she explain that there was no other way but to obey the Master's orders?

Nell realizing the servant had no choice; assumed all responsibility by saying she would talk with her father-in-law. LaBelle, still troubled, left shaking her head.

"Clydette let us go downstairs to pick up books," Nell called her aide, who ran to follow her going down the stairs. When reaching the lower floor, Nell saw the woman who had helped LaBelle cleaning at the other end of the room. Cecil's office was closed; the Master must be out inspecting the plantation or visiting friends or associates. Nell and Clydette entered the mansion's small library.

A moment later, Wade came through a back door; walking slowly, grabbed the cleaning servant from behind. Covering her mouth, he pulled her into a room at the end of the hall.

"Darlene, was she your fiancée?" Nell asked, combing her hair at a mirror. Gabriel getting dressed a few steps away, was surprised by the unexpected question. Nell watched him through the mirror, appearing as calm as possible.

"Who told you?"

"It does not matter. Please, answer my question."

"Yes, long ago," he said with low voice, evidently not happy to remember it.

"Why didn't you tell me?"

"What importance has it now? It is something from the past, where it should remain." Visibly disturbed, Gabriel came to the mirror, pretending to check his hair.

"I was curious. She is a constant visitor. I wanted to know her relationship with your family," Nell explained as serenely as she could; put the hairbrush on the counter and checked her hairdo.

"The engagement was arranged by our parents," Gabriel said, looking at Nell in the mirror. He had wanted to avoid any discussion with his wife related to his past romantic life, but now he had no choice. "We became sweethearts at an early age. Fortunately, when we realized we were not in love, we ended the engagement by mutual consent." His voice was strong as he finished, clearly relieved to have cleared the air.

"I am glad I did not experience such an imposition from my family," Nell confessed.

"To accept the breakup was not easy for our parents. Both families had put their hopes in our union, but they could not force us. I am grateful to Darlene because she agreed to end our engagement; we became good friends with no bitterness between us. She continues to be close to my mother which is convenient for everybody."

"Yes, your mother needs company," Nell observed.

"I agree," Gabriel answered, relaxed now that it seemed the subject did not disturb his wife. "Ready to go down?"

Moving toward the door, he offered his hand, inviting Nell to follow him. The couple left the room, entering the hall connecting with the spiral stairway. The noise of shutting a door made them to look at the other side. It was Cecil leaving his apartment. He walked toward them; Gabriel and Nell waited for him. She glanced at her father-in-law, who was impeccably dressed as usual. Even though he was not as stout, tall as Gabriel, his strong personality compensated the physical differences between them. As they came downstairs, Nell mentioned to her in-law it was not necessary Clydette being at her door long after night. Cecil did not answer which Nell interpreted as he had accepted her decision. Anne and Edna left her downstairs apartment, joining the group as they entered the dining room. Each of them sat at their habitual seats. LaBelle and other servants walked in with food; dinner was served.

"Anne," Cecil said, bringing a napkin to his lips. Automatically, everyone raised their heads, paying attention to the head of the household. "Stop seeing that boy," he ordered with firm tone. Cecil continued eating as did everybody else. After dinner, the reunion in the private parlor did not last long. Everyone wanted to retire. Once in their bedroom, Nell questioned Gabriel about what his father said to Anne but Gabriel was completely unaware about it. Nell finished combing her hair and left the room, crossing the hall to Anne's place. She gently knocked on the door; the young woman answered and invited her to come inside. Immediately Nell questioned her: "Who are you seeing that your father disapproves?"

"Anson," the young woman said, sitting on the bed.

Nell came closer. By now she already knew Cecil's opinions were difficult to ignore and dangerous to rebut. "When do you see him?"

"After leaving school, when walking to the buggy. Wade probably saw us."

Nell sat next to her. The situation was not so bad but precaution was imperative. "Be careful," Nell warned.

The girl objected, "Why can't we talk? He is so pleasant. I feel good in his company."

"You are doing nothing shameful but your father's approval is crucial. My advice is to stop meeting Anson; that will increase your image in your father's eyes. Later, if you still want to see him, try to overcome his opposition. After some time, perhaps he will not have objection."

"I don't know, Nell. Father does not change his mind easily."

"That is true but to disobey him will not help. Tomorrow is a different day. Believe me; I am older."

"Thanks, Nell," Anne said embracing her. "I will do as you say."

"You can always count on my support," Nell assured her sister-in-law before returning to her chambers.

Dissension

LaBelle came to Nell's room without assistant and asked for Clydette to help her.

"Where is the other woman?" Nell inquired.

"Miss Nell, she is sick," LaBelle answered, not looking at her.

Nell gave her permission. When the room was done, LaBelle solicited Clydette to continue helping. She had many places to take care of and could not get another slave.

Today more than the usual number of visitors came to Cecil's office. The steady noise of walking and loud voices filled the entrance hall. Unexpectedly, Gabriel came home early, his face troubled.

"My dear, we are in a delicate position," he said holding his wife's hands. "Opposition to slavery is increasing among Northern politicians. A few Southern states are considering seceding from the Union. We are a small community and must follow the majority. There is a town meeting tonight to discuss the crisis. Every citizen of Roseville will attend with their families, as is usual when a major problem arises. Father, Anne and I will be there; it is important you to come."

"Of course I'll go," Nell confirmed.

The Gilberts' carriage entered town. The coachman, instructed by Wade sitting at his side, pulled the reins to lessen the horse's pace. People walked through the muddy road because the plank sidewalks were full, holding the traffic.

"I did not know Roseville had so many inhabitants," Nell commented, looking around.

"This matter affects everyone," Gabriel explained. "Nobody will miss this call."

Upon arriving at the meeting house, Wade opened the door for his Masters. Cecil came out of the carriage followed by Anne and Aunt Mabel. Gabriel was next, helping Nell to step down. The Gilberts walked into a big room, already crowded. Nell, holding hands with Gabriel followed her father-in-law going straight, stopping at a set of long benches, seats evidently reserved for certain people. They sat gazing around; saluting with head nods and hand waves others nearby or across the way.

Everyone was talking excitedly. A gallery encircled the benches, giving an interesting tone to the gathering. The occupants of the balcony, probably less prominent citizens, Nell guessed from their shabbier looking clothes, seemed equally concerned. She had never seen anything like this, her eyes going from one place to the next. She was impressed, and somehow scared.

"Hi!"

The loud, friendly voice made Nell to come back from her thoughts. It was Darlene and her parents. The young woman, as usual, was smiling as she embraced everybody with her particular, familiar gesture. Only Cecil reciprocated her with the same enthusiasm. Dexter and parents also joined them, sitting next to Darlene and family. Their greetings were short because in the middle of the room, an old gentleman was raising arms, calling for everyone's attention. After he received complete silence, he addressed them:

"Ladies, gentlemen, citizens of Roseville: we are here tonight not to announce good news as we generally do," the speaker said calmly but with a noticeably sad tone, swiveling his head around to look at everyone. "I believe you have read recently many opinions published against us . . . our happy life, should I add."

A general clamor of assent ran through the assembly.

"Unfortunately," the speaker continued when silence returned, "each time more aggressive, negative arguments against our institutions are presented. Our neighbors are considering secession. We, of Roseville, are not a legally separate county.

Therefore, we must follow their decision, which reminds us of the importance of becoming a municipality. Then, we could manage our own affairs."

He sat down. A general discussion started between various groups. Nell observed the crowd. She remembered the first orator. He had attended her presentation ball. Then, Cecil Gilbert stood. Gradually, the voices ended and everyone's attention concentrated on the new orator.

"I completely agree with Judge Davis," Cecil began with his natural, habitual calm. "Roseville must become a municipality. We have the population and the economic power." He looked around at the people, near and far, and then continued. "To those outsiders talking about abolitionism, they should remember that the federal government has no authority over slavery. Only Slave States could legally end it."

Unanimous approval from the public followed those words. One after other, people stood up, cheerfully applauding. Cecil, smiling, took a bow giving his thanks for the noisy reaction. He sat down. A few nearby men came and congratulated him personally. The following participants voiced the group's consensus:

"We will not surrender this prosperous land."

"Slavery is their natural condition. They are happy, better off enslaved."

"We will defend our borders."

"Northern abolitionists are lunatics."

"Emancipation would bring social chaos."

"It's better to secede than give our way of life."

"Yes! Yes!" came shouts from the gallery, rising into a rebellious cry.

"War . . . War!" somebody yelled from the background, increasing the crowd's defiant mood. The straightforward arguments hit both mind and soul of the common and gentle Southerners. A cold chill ran through Nell. The theme dominated the meeting, many speakers insisting on taking radical actions if necessary to guard their beloved land. A chaotic discussion developed, everyone angrily expressing their strong convictions. Then Cecil stood up again. Gesturing, he asked for everyone's attention. After a few seconds, more and more people calmed, the well-known Master Gilbert addressed the audience: "We favor our rights to maintain our system and have heard insistently the idea of war, secession." He paused, looking out over the crowd. "Yet if we separate, we will lose all constitutional guarantees, including the fugitive slaves' law. Also, we have no army. Adopting extreme measures is dangerous. We must find practical, suitable solutions." Cecil sat. This time, the response was not a favorable one. Loud, angry voices in the background clearly indicated that. Group discussions started. Then a tall, middle-aged man, standing, gained the general attention.

"This new Republican Party, their candidate for president, 'Abram' Lincoln, is he not against slavery in the new territories? If elected, will he not liberate the slaves?"

A collective murmur ran among the listeners. Nell was troubled, disbelieving the massive uproar that so easily overran the crowd, the gallery particularly. She looked around, astonished. *Isn't that young man over there Anson? He surely is,* she thought as her eyes scanned the balcony.

Another person from upstairs added his thoughts: "To free the slaves would bring social monstrosities: robberies, murders of whites, blacks chasing white women. There is no doubt. If necessary, we must form a new nation and even go to war against the North to preserve our land and properties."

Everybody warmly agreed, except Nell, who so far had tried hard to accept the differences between her culture and this one, to be in compliance with the institution she disagreed with. She came from a Free State, where blacks and whites live in harmony, and she wondered where the speaker's lugubrious predictions came from. A new speaker stood, this time from downstairs:

"Is not a Northerner among us?" the man asked, looking at the Gilberts.

"My wife is above suspicion!" Gabriel, standing up firmly answered.

An uncomfortable sensation went through the Gilbert family and friends. After all, was not the speaker's doubt too premature? Anyway, what could she do against them? Never since moving South had Nell felt so uneasy. The questioner, sensing his words had brought an unwelcome subject, sat. But Nell stood, surprising not only her companions, but all present. Rapidly the attention of the attendants concentrated on her.

"My name is Nell," she started, her voice a little shaky. "My husband is Gabriel Gilbert, here at my side; and yes, I am from the North."

The audience remained almost completely silent, showing interest in this "foreigner."

"When I came to be part of this family, I moved to Roseville," Nell continued, now more confident. "In doing so, I became a Southerner." Her last words, tone firm.

Aunt Mabel nodded while looking around. Loud voices of approval came from listeners close and far, showing acceptance for and supporting the young woman.

"If we go to war, what side you will be on?" a man asked. A tense silence hung over the crowded hall.

"I will be neutral," Nell affirmed.

Her relatives showed signs of agreement, though that answer did not please others, judging by the choir of mumbled utterances. When the clamor died down, Nell explained: "I oppose war."

That position seemed acceptable to many, although somebody wanted details. "Do you mean all kinds of war, Mrs. Gilbert, The Revolutionary War?"

Nell faced the man who questioned her. Then, moving her attention to the public, she said: "Ask a war widow, a mother who lost her only son what she thinks about wars."

Silence followed. The audience was surprised by the striking arguments given by the new citizen. Nell and Gabriel sat. People commented the subject but soon was forgotten, returning the discussion mainly to the possibility of secession, each speaker maintaining his conviction. After a period passed where no one added any new idea or solution, Judge Davis proposed to end the meeting, assuring he would call for another reunion if anything new concerning the matter developed. Besides, since a great majority of the citizens seemed to be in agreement with the idea of secession, no action is needed.

Afterward, a gloomy ambience descended over Roseville. Cecil's office was visited almost daily by the judge, Dexter's, Darlene's father, plus others who were not frequently there. The discussions were at times so loud that they could be heard from the entrance hall to adjacent rooms. Nell could easily recognize many faces she had seen at the meeting or the presentation ball.

Gabriel was busy too, often traveling out of town or returning home late. If Nell questioned him, he always answered without saying much, sounding pessimistic. LaBelle, also, was not as friendly as she used to be. When asked a question or to do something, she responded ceremoniously. Even with other slaves she was stern, hurrying them, leaving the room immediately after her task was finished. Nell opted not to pay too much heed to any of this. Her mentality was that crisis comes and goes, and even this would eventually pass.

Nell, sitting at the window saw Anne coming from school escorted by Wade walking directly into Cecil's office. That was strange; the young lady never visited her father at that time. Nell stood, watching curiously. Wade closed the door after Anne, walked down the long hall and left through the back door.

Nell turned her attention to Clydette who was placing clothing into a drawer of the commode. She was retiring from the window when a scream came from downstairs. Nell froze. A loud discussion followed between daughter and father, their voices disorderly as one shouted over the other. The tension increased with each yell with no trace of an end. Moved by the desire to help her surrogate sister, Nell rushed downstairs. Edna opened her door just as Nell reached the ground floor. Undecided, the older woman stood there, watching Nell going straight to the place of action. Determined, Nell knocked, then immediately turned the knob, opened the office's door. Entering the room, it took a quick look to give her a disturbing picture. Cecil, seated in the executive chair, his arms over the desk. He was red-faced and perspiring. Anne, sitting in a chair across from him, was shaking and crying.

"You disobeyed my order not to see that boy!"

"I am doing nothing wrong," the girl answered.

"You will go to school no more, nor leave this house without my permission!" Cecil shouted.

"I am not a child!" she retorted.

"Anne, please don't argue with your father," Nell intervened, hoping to end the exchange of angry words. "Please, Mr. Gilbert, let me take Anne out. She is in very bad shape," Nell pleaded, looking at him. Without waiting for an answer, she raised Anne from the chair and walked toward the exit.

"You will not disobey me again, or my name is not Cecil Gilbert!" the man thundered, watching the women depart.

Once in the hall, Edna directed them into her rooms and then closed the door.

"Daughter, do not confront your father," Edna pleaded. "You know how he is." She sat her daughter down on the sofa. Nell stood close.

"Mother, he is a fine boy," Anne insisted still crying. "We are not doing anything shameful."

"I know, Anne, but that is not enough for your father," Edna said.

"He will not let me go to school! Mother, it's my last year and I want to graduate."

Edna looked at her sorrowful face. She wanted to help but since the master of the house was involved, nothing she could do.

"Anne, I will talk to Mr. Gilbert. You will go back and finish your education," Nell said confident Cecil would reverse the drastic, hasty decision he had made. Edna stared at Nell, wondering, *Does she seriously think he will listen to her?*

That night, Nell informed Gabriel about the dispute between Anne and her father and that she had promised to speak to him on Anne's behalf. She asked for her husband's support. He promised would back her up, but suggested not to bring up the matter at dinnertime because his father disliked discussions at the table. At dinner, Nell verified that it was not the appropriate time to present the plea. Nobody was in a friendly mood, and scarcely anyone spoke at all.

The next day, Nell went to Cecil's office when he was alone. She entreated him with her most ample smile, and then sat facing him. Immediately she made the request, emphasizing the importance for Anne to finish school. The response: a flat refusal. Cecil made no compromise and would not have any discussion of any aspect of the matter. He made it clear that nothing would change the master's ruling; it was surely closed. A sad feeling overcame Nell. The rough decision made by Mr. Gilbert without listening to reasons served as an important lesson for caution in the future.

In the following days, the mansion was a silent, cold place, even with Anne around the house. The young lady spent most of her time inside her chambers. Nell visited her frequently, developing a more solid friendship with the girl. Occasionally both women went to the front garden, enjoying fine weather. However, that also was restricted since Anson was spotted outside, on the road to the estate. Wade was charged with keeping the boy off the premises.

It was not a week later that somebody knocked on the mansion's front door. Wade, on his way out, opened it. A tall, thin, middle-aged man hurriedly burst in and walked toward Cecil's private office. The plantation owner, reading the *Charleston Mercury* newspaper, put it down. The visitor, agitated, took his stovepipe hat off, revealing disheveled hair.

"Why can't my son see your daughter?" he exploded suddenly, looking straight at Cecil.

Who is he that dares to speak to me like this? the man wondered. Standing up, Cecil confronted the intruder.

"I need not to give you any explanation!" and that was all he would say, but the authoritarian voice did not intimidate the other man.

"My son is suffering!"

That argument broke Cecil's patience. "Get *out!*" he yelled but his order was not obeyed.

"We are poor but honest," the man riposted, "and have no problems with the law!"

This insolent man had gone too far. "WADE!" the Master yelled. The loyal man hurried in. Confronted with expulsion, the uninvited guest angrily put his hat on and pushing Wade aside quickly left.

The atmosphere at the Gilberts' house, already tense, worsened. That night Gabriel told Nell about the incident with Anson's father.

Where was I to miss that? she wondered.

"He had the audacity to question Father," Gabriel told her.

"Oh, God. What did he say?"

"Not much . . . he is poor but honest." Gabriel moved around, visibly uncomfortable. "He should have known that coming here would not help. I must talk to Anne. This is getting out of control."

Nell agreed. Before dinner they stopped at Anne's room. The young woman opened the door and invited them to come in giving the last touch to her dressing.

"Anne, this boy Anson," Gabriel said directly, "his father came today."

She was surprised to hear this.

"This is becoming a little complicated," Gabriel continued. "This behavior does more harm than good to both sides."

Visibly disturbed, Anne sat on the bed, tears running down her cheeks.

"We want to help," Nell assured, sitting at her side and holding her hands.

"I did nothing wrong and yet Father does not let me go to finish school," she protested.

"Anne, I did not graduate either, but for different reason," Nell explained, trying to ease her sister-in-law's worries. She went on in a low, friendly tone to describe her experience. "My last year it snowed so hard that the roads were impassible. When spring came, conditions better but it was too late. I never went back. But here, at home, we have books you can read and improve your knowledge," she added. "Not long ago I read in the library about the defeat of the Spanish Invincible Armada by Sir Francis Drake. There are also texts describing the Renaissance, religious wars, and many other things. If you are interested, I am ready to help. You just pick the topic, and we'll study it."

"That would be great," Gabriel agreed, adding, "Since the weather is good now you can read in the garden."

"Thanks," Anne said, "but we'll have to do it here, in my rooms. Father does not let me going out."

Gabriel was taken aback.

Nell explained, "Anson has been seen around. Cecil ordered Anne not to leave the house."

"Ridiculous!" Gabriel exclaimed, "Anne cannot be always inside. Anyway, he will never dare to come to the gardens. I will talk to Father."

"You already know he was firm in his decision about Anne going back to school when I talked to him," Nell reminded her husband.

"Yes, but this is too much. Anne is not a prisoner." Gabriel was determined to intercede, to fight for his sister and get a favorable solution.

The next day in Cecil's office, Gabriel and Wade were discussing duties with the head of the plantation. Cecil ordered Wade to do some routine work and to check the merchandise that in a few weeks would be sent to Boston for shipment to Europe. Gabriel already had his instructions but he kept listening, waiting. After all routine business matters were taken care of, Wade wanted to talk about a situation in the fields.

"Mr. Gilbert, a slave girl is missing," Wade informed him. "The rumors are not good."

"A runaway?" Gabriel asked.

"I don't think so," Wade responded.

Cecil inquired, "Then, what is it?"

"She and her boyfriend disappeared a few days ago. Now he is back saying knows nothing about her."

"These people always causing problems," the Master complained.

"Lately, the missing girl used to help LaBelle in the mansion," Wade continued.

"Well," Cecil instructed, "if she does not show up, report her to the authorities."

Wade nodded and, business taken care of, walked to the door. He stopped, waiting for Gabriel.

"I will see you outside," he told him. Wade left.

"I heard Anne is not allowed to go to the garden," Gabriel stated directly. "This is not a too harsh prohibition for a grown up woman?"

Cecil raised his eyes. For the first time his son questioned his decisions. Controlling his temper, he patiently listened to Gabriel's arguments. The young man advocated for Anne, saying that due her age, already sixteen, it was surely time to allow some saying in matters concerning her life. Besides, Nell will be there too. Gabriel's truthful plea left no doubt. Cecil capitulated, lifting the prohibition but cautioning that he still would not tolerate disobedience about seeing Anson. Satisfied, Gabriel thanked him and left. Outside the office, at the entrance he saw Dexter coming. Mr. Gilbert, he said, had sent for him. Gabriel nodded and continued to Anne's chambers, where the women gladly received the good news.

Promptly Anne and Nell scheduled study sessions in the garden. On their way out, Nell picked up a book from the mansion's library related to the Renaissance, the subject requested by Anne.

"Isn't it amazing? These men, discovering the world's secrets kept hidden so long and creating those fabulous works of art?"

"Yes, Nell. And during a time when scientific investigation did not exist."

"Science studies were born during those years, teaching that no matter how weird an idea seems, if one followed it till the end the results would probably surprise even the person experimenting."

The radiant midday sun made them seek refuge in the pavilion. Clydette stayed out in the sunshine, chasing butterflies. The approaching of a horseman caught their attention. It was Dexter.

"Having a good time?" Dismounting, he saluted the ladies.

"What are you doing here?" Anne asked.

"I saw you and dropped by."

"Thanks, Dexter," Anne answered. She explained their presence in the garden, inviting him to join. He accepted, surprising Anne and Nell too. They discussed the Renaissance at length.

These lessons benefited both women. Nell got to review old knowledge and keeping busy, not having a bored moment, made the days to pass faster. Besides, Anne's company was a positive factor because it helped to complete the adaptation to her new life in the South. Anne gained too because Nell was a patient companion. The sister-figure's guidance matured Anne intellect and character.

"I'm glad my queen is happy," Gabriel said, buttoning his shirt as he stood behind Nell at a mirror. She was smiling, putting the last touches to her hairdo.

"It was a great idea to get Anne and me together. We are now close friends."

"I can see it. Tell me, besides interesting reading, what else you do?"

"Gabriel, she is intelligent. In a short time we read about the Crusades, Sir Isaac Newton, Aristotle and Archimedes."

"Slow down, you are going to fast! Who are those characters?" he joked.

"C'mon, you know what I'm talking about."

"How have you covered all that? Does our library carry such a number of cultural texts?"

"Very simply. Subjects we don't have at hand we order them from Roseville's store. Clydette picks them up."

"Excellent! I'm glad to discover how resourceful my wife is." He kissed her neck.

"And Dexter sometimes joins us," Nell said. Gabriel was surprised to hear this but he took it in stride.

That afternoon, Anne was smiling more than usual. Nell did not question her, instead simply directing the reading as they regularly did. Today Galileo Galilei was the biography chosen.

"Wasn't he a miraculous person who could learn that much by himself?"

"Yes," Nell agreed. "Equally interesting Anne was that some of his discoveries made with rudimentary instruments still prove true to this day."

"It would be satisfactory but frightening to have such an inquisitive mind."

"And in those years it was dangerous to disagree with the establishment as Galileo did."

"Nevertheless Nell, the truth prevailed."

"But it was not easy. Galileo was questioned by the Inquisition, something very damaging for anybody. Yet contrary to general belief, there is no proof that he insisted the Earth does move."

Anne shook her head. "Surely that was an unfortunate day for him."

"Yes. But as you said, Galileo's achievements were eventually found certain and widely accepted, confirming that knowledge will always prevail against ignorance."

They were distracted by the noise of a horse coming. Again, Dexter was stepping into the garden.

"Anne, let's go for a ride," he invited. "It is a beautiful day."

"Thanks, Dexter, but I'm busy."

"Miss Nell will let you go. You have to have some fun too, you know," Dexter insisted holding the horse.

Anne replied tersely, "Another day. I am not prepared for horse riding right now."

"Then will you come for a walk? I like to talk . . . if Miss Nell does not oppose."

"Anne is free to do whatever she wishes," Nell quickly responded, clearing her of responsibility, leaving such a decision to Anne. Since the reading session was over she had no reason but to accept the invitation.

"I am going back to the mansion. Please, Anne, come inside when possible," Nell said, picking up the books and walking toward the entrance followed by Clydette. Anne and Dexter went the other way, walking around the well-attended garden.

"This is a gorgeous place," Dexter said admiring the flowers and bushes around.

"Nell's idea."

"Anne, you know me well. I have been thinking, trying to talk . . . " He was hesitant.

"Dexter, do you have a problem?"

"No . . . I hope you understand . . . agree with me."

"About what?"

"If you say yes, I'll ask your father's permission to marry you," he finally managed to say.

Anne stopped walking. Overall she could imagine such thought had never crossed her mind.

"Dexter, I've known you all my life. You and my brother Gabriel are very close; you are like family, a very good friend . . . "

"Will you consider my proposal?" he hurriedly interrupted, hoping to distract the negative response he sensed was coming.

"I have nothing to think about, Dexter. You are a terrific young man but I could never marry you."

"Anne, please I beg you. I'll wait as long as you wish."

"Sorry, Dexter. You already know my answer." Turning, Anne came back to the mansion.

Wade and Gabriel's regular morning meeting with Cecil Gilbert went as usual. They discussed the daily chores. At the end Cecil, worried by the increasing tension between the North and the South, said it would be convenient to improve the living conditions of the slaves to soothe the 'alarming' idea of emancipation that was going through the plantations. Consequently, he asked Gabriel and Wade to designate areas between the regular crops where the slaves could plant vegetables and fruit trees for them. Gabriel was proud; after all, the master *was* concerned about his servants too. He and Wade left the office and went outside. There, two slaves holding horses waited for them. As Gabriel was ready to get up, Dexter arrived. Dismounting, he waved a greeting before going into the mansion. A curious feeling invaded Gabriel. Following a sudden impulse, he told Wade to go on ahead and he came back to the mansion. He heard voices coming from the office. Dexter was there. Gabriel opened the door.

"I tried, Mr. Gilbert." The young man standing was talking to Cecil. "But Anne."

Gabriel's presence interrupted the conversation. Visibly nervous, Dexter looked at him.

"What is going on?" Gabriel asked. Both men were too surprised to answer immediately. "Father, will you please tell me?" Gabriel insisted.

"Nothing to worry about, son," Cecil answered, recovering his serene pose. "There is a misunderstanding, Gabriel. I will take care of it."

"I want to know." His tone left no doubt. Cecil looked at Dexter, then at his son.

"Dexter proposed to Anne. She rejected him."

A look of concern instantly appeared on Gabriel's face. "Father, do not do it again. Remember what happened with my arranged engagement to Darlene? Please, leave Anne alone."

That day, Anne requested not to read, just to walk. Accordingly, the two women strolled between the bushes and roses in bloom. Anne was uncommonly happy, smiling. Nell had noticed a change in her attitude days ago, but today it was clear something was out of the ordinary. Approaching a bench, Nell sat; Anne kept going around while Clydette ran along the trail, singing.

"I don't want to be indiscreet, Anne. You are all smiles!"

"Why you say that?" the girl asked, turning around and facing her mentor with a grin on her face.

"Frankly, my dear, since we have been together, I have not seen you . . . so happy."

"You are right, Nell. I've never felt so good in my life!"

Nell returned her smiles. "I am so glad for you."

"Nell, I must tell you." Coming over, the girl sat next to her. "Anson loves me!"

This surprised Nell. "Anne, do not go so fast."

"I am not. He told me."

"Oh, my God! Things are getting complicated. But you have not gone into Roseville in weeks. How do you know this?"

"He sent me a letter. He promised to love me always."

"Dear, I will not say anything against that, but be careful," Nell warned, a worried look upon her face. "You say he sent a letter?"

"Yes. He gave it to Clydette when she went to pick up books."

"Oh, I see," Nell said, standing up. She started to fear that her unwanted participation in this matter could damage her relations with the Gilberts.

"This is the best love-letter ever written," Anne added following Nell. "He says someday, somehow he will walk through this entrance trail and take me away!" As she said this she raised her arms up to the air and run toward the main road; in her eyes the vision of a young medieval rider knight coming to rescue her. Nell faced the smiling girl and, wanting to share such confidence embraced her. Holding hands, both women walked up and down the garden paths, again and again, one with a heart full of joy, the other with feelings of caution inside. Soon the sun disappeared under a dark, stormy sky. Raindrops starting falling forcing Nell, Anne and Clydette to rush inside the mansion. A heavy storm hit Roseville that afternoon. Back in her apartments, Nell had to hold Clydette who was dreadfully afraid of lightning and thunder. LaBelle came around, checking every room, and took away the young slave saying she should not annoy her Master. The electrical storm made even Cecil Gilbert close the curtain over the window with a view to the main gate since the lightning flashes constantly interrupted his attention.

Gabriel and Wade were in the field, checking the new cotton gin just put into service, when the storm hit. They hurriedly ordered to shut doors and windows of the shelter. The lightning and thunder alarmed young slave girls, who embraced older women, standing motionless under the heavy rain. Gabriel told Wade to dismiss them to their quarters but the foreman did not agree; he reminded the young master they were slaves and rain and mud were "natural" elements for them. Gabriel opted not to press the matter; anyway, field work was Wade's territory. Instead, he went to his horse parked outside the shelter, took a raincoat from the saddlebag, and put it on. Mounting his horse, he left, guessing Wade would do likewise. The slaves, left alone would take refuge from the storm.

Back in the mansion, Gabriel was received with wide-open arms by Nell. She was really impressed by the storm, the first one she'd experienced since moving South.

At the next morning's meeting, Cecil asked, "How is the cotton gin machine functioning? Do they know how to operate it?"

"So far, there is little problem putting it into production," responded Wade.

"This is something completely new for them and us, too," Gabriel added. "Wade is training them. Soon, they will be operating it without supervision. They are learning faster than anticipated."

"Keep an eye on them; they're lazy," reminded the Master. "Wade, any news about the missing slave?"

"Somebody saw her around, but no details, Sir. You know how they are, talk very little, many times you can't understand what they say," Wade reported.

"Did you inform the authorities?"

"No, Sir. I am waiting; maybe we'll hear anything about her."

"If two more days pass and she does not appear, report her."

"Yes, Mr. Gilbert." With that the meeting broke up.

Wade, surrounded by a few male slaves, gave instructions on how to operate the ginning machine. Gabriel, on his horse, observed at a distance in case to be of any assistance. Wade's explanations were not always accurate, since he was still unfamiliar with the machine, too; it was a novelty to all. At times, his words did not match the function he was trying to describe. Besides, the illiterate audience could barely understand and the handy employee made no effort to be understood.

Suddenly, the gathering was distracted by the shouting of an old slave coming out the surrounding forest: "Dead, in 'dar' bushes!"

The slaves ran to meet him. What was he talking about? Almost without breath, the old slave fell in the arms of others, repeating that there was a 'dead body' in the woods. Gabriel rode toward the group and inquired where he had seen it.

"'Suh, atter' those trees," the man replied, pointing to the forest.

Gabriel guided his horse to the zone indicated, being followed by the slaves. Wade, leaving the warehouse, began walking slowly in their direction. Gabriel, reaching the spot, got off his horse. There, behind thick, tall bushes laid a body. Bending to his knees, the young man cautiously inspected it. It was a female; a big blood spot on her chest. There were no signs of life present.

The crowd of slaves stood a few yards away, gawking at the young woman's body on the ground. Gabriel took a second look; her face was familiar. He also noticed she was pregnant. "Anybody knows her?" he questioned, turning to the group. Silence. They were too afraid and accustomed to remain silent but on their faces were indications that they did know her.

"Wade, come closer. Do you recognize her?"

He walked toward Gabriel. After a quick view of the body, he turned his head.

"She is the runaway slave," Wade identified her with low, emotionless voice.

"Are you sure?"

"Yes, Gabriel." The firmness in his tone left no doubt.

"Evidently, she was murdered. The wound on her lower chest . . . blood is still fresh. This happened not long ago, but who could do this . . . why?" Gabriel said, moved by the tragic event. The slaves around Gabriel did not say a word. Their eyes, accustomed to gracelessness showed little emotion. Wade moved a few steps away. This was not the first slave found murdered on a Southern plantation. Gabriel asked again if anyone knew the woman and was interested in advising her relatives who wanted to take care of the corpse, but no one answered. Instead, they just started walking away. Suddenly a young black man came running from the forest waving a machete. He headed directly to Wade and slashed at the overseer's shoulder, producing a deep cut. The slaves ran in all directions, avoiding the attacker. Wade, stepping back, pulled out a small gun he had on his waist belt. He fired but the bullet went into the air, since off balance he fell to the ground. Gabriel rushed to Wade's side while the attacker ran back into the forest in the confusion of the tumult. Gabriel helped Wade to stand up; blood was coming from his shoulder.

"Can you ride?"

"Yes, Gabriel. Don't worry."

They went to Wade's horse under the curious eyes of a few coming back spectators. Gabriel pulled out a string from the saddlebag and fastened it around Wade's arm as tight as possible. Then the young man helped the employee mount his horse.

"You need medical treatment. I will escort you." Gabriel indicated. He climbed onto his horse and guided the animal to the road followed by Wade.

The news of the day's incidents rapidly spread around the nearby plantations and mansions, not because the death of a slave but because where it had happened. Gilbert's slaves were always peaceful and obedient. Also, the attack of a white man by a slave was highly disturbing.

When Gabriel arrived back at the mansion, he went directly to inform his father. Cecil was furious. How this could happen, this slave dared to injure the master's representative? Gabriel could not answer these or other questions the angry owner had. The only thing he knew was that it did take place; he had witnessed it with his own eyes.

Gabriel reported that Wade was now resting safely in his cabin after receiving medical treatment in the nearby city. He also told his father that the slain slave woman was the runaway one. This didn't interest much Mr. Gilbert; the challenge of his authority was his main concern. Nothing Gabriel may say could calm him.

The news worried Nell, too, once she heard about it that night. Slaves or not, human beings' tragedy always impressed and saddened her.

"Miss Nell, I need Clydette," LaBelle requested the next morning when she entered Nell's chambers. "Today I could not get help; all the young women are busy."

Nell raised her eyes from the book she was reading. The slave woman was uncommonly serious, surely because of the events that had just occurred.

"Clydette, come. Help LaBelle."

Smiling, the young slave joined in doing the chores around the room. LaBelle talked only when needed to. Once the cleaning was completed, both servants left.

Nell could not concentrate on reading. She went out to Anne's apartment and knocked on the door. At the girl's invitation, she opened it and walked inside. Anne was on a couch, sitting under a window, her face joyful. Nell sat close to her. The previous day's events came rapidly into their conversation, mainly the murdered slave who had worked with LaBelle. They remembered seeing a girl but were unable to visualize her face. Anyway, both lamented the young slave woman's death and wondered why Wade was attacked. Maybe, due to his job; after all, he surely had enemies in the working fields.

"Let us change the subject," Nell suggested. "I received a new book about the Invincible Armada. That could be the subject of our next reading session."

"I have news for you, too," Anne said. "Anson sent another letter!"

The information made Nell happy, but also uneasy. This secret correspondence was dangerous. Anne went on. "He no longer works for M. Pierre. His father got for him a job with the pharmacist; he will train Anson in preparation of medicines."

"That is marvelous, Anne. It is important to learn a profession."

"And this is not all, Nell. He is studying at night to improve his education."

"This young man really amazes me," Nell said, impressed.

"I am so happy, Nell. Surely he will do all he says," a confident Anne assured.

Nell smiled, still torn between happiness for her sister-in-law and the uneasy feeling of disobeying Cecil's orders.

All that week, LaBelle was unable to get helpers for work around the mansion even though it was an esteemed privilege to work there. Nell figured she simply was not trying hard to replace the murdered girl. Therefore, Clydette became the only one LaBelle could count on. Mr. Gilbert was not interested in the matter and Nell did not complain Clydette was no longer her companion. Anyway, she is learning to become a good housekeeper which would benefit her as the lectures and advices Nell provided in the afternoons during the reading in the garden whenever possible.

For these reasons, Nell did not want to completely lose Clydette; there was much still to teach her.

Because of this, Nell said one morning, "LaBelle, send Clydette to me when she finished with the housekeeping."

The slave woman assented, "Miss Nell, you know how big this mansion is. We have no free moments."

"I am sure you can release her sometime."

"If you ask, Miss Nell, of course Clydette can be with you when you want," she responded.

"LaBelle, I will not argue with you. I just want her to continue learning to read and write."

"She needs not that."

"I cannot believe it," Nell answered, almost angry. "You learned how to read and write. Why not Clydette?"

"It is different. She will not take care of the mansion," LaBelle affirmed.

"I see no reason why she could not. Of course, if she is not allowed to learn she will continue to be a simple servant."

"She is a slave and always will be," LaBelle said stoically.

"Nevertheless, if she reads and writes she could get a higher position like you," Nell insisted.

"Lucky I Master Edna Gilbert taught me. But with Clydette it will not happen."

"Why not? I want to teach her and you should agree with me. You know you are in better conditions than those in the cotton fields."

"Working in the mansion is no longer good," LaBelle answered looking straight at the Master with tears suddenly steaming down her face.

"What?" Nell asked somehow confused.

"Nothing; I say no more." Cleaning her face LaBelle turned away.

"What do you mean 'not good'?"

Almost crying again LaBelle answered, "Miss Nell, you know . . . the woman who worked here, her boyfriend killed her."

"That is ridiculous. Because she worked here, was killed?"

"Miss Nell, not like that. You see, she was pregnant."

"So he did not want her to continue working in the mansion," Nell reasoned.

"Oh, God! It is not how you say, Miss Nell!"

"To me, it makes no sense."

LaBelle moved around, wishing to escape the trap into which she had fallen. But Nell had been so kind to her, nobody had treated her so well. Therefore, she revealed the troubling truth: "Miss Nell, the slave was pregnant not by her boyfriend . . . but by someone else."

"That is disturbing, LaBelle," Nell said worriedly.

"He asked her to run away with him; he came from another plantation, not Master Gilbert's . . . now he is missing," LaBelle finished short of breath.

Nell kept silent. The loyal slave rushed out the room.

Nell told Gabriel her conversation with LaBelle. He already knew the male slave did not belong to them. His owner had already reported him as a runaway. He reminded her that these problems were not new and with time she would learn not to worry much about such things.

A few days later, Wade informed his employer that the aggressor slave, the murderer of the female slave had been found dead, hung, apparently by himself in Gilbert's territory. The news spread rapidly and the 'incident' was soon 'forgotten'.

LaBelle's behavior worsened. She gave instructions grudgingly and talked in the most unfriendly tone. Though not happy with this behavior, Nell looked the other way when it happened in her presence, hoping that the trusted servant would change her mood and manners once the pain and frustration caused by the death of someone she knew faded.

Reviewing a book she had taken from the downstairs library, Nell came back to her apartment in the middle of the morning.

"You must do it; I'll tell you how!"

LaBelle, close to Clydette, was talking softly; stopped and they moved apart upon seeing Nell. This attitude intrigued her, but she kept her pace pretending she had not heard. Once inside the bedroom, she sat and started reading the book, gazing blankly at the pages while on the other side of the room LaBelle's talking to Clydette resumed. Nell stood up, walked to the end of the bedroom making sure she was seen and then returned along close to the wall, unseen, toward the parlor. She kept next to the lintel, paying attention to the next room. Now the words clearly reached her:

"I'll help you to get to Jacksonville. You will travel by night, but do not be afraid . . . "

Nell did not need to hear more. *How could loyal LaBelle be promoting this dangerous, unlawful thing?* she wondered. During these past long months that Clydette had been at her service, affection had developed between them. Also, to engage a young, inexperienced person in such a dangerous activity with so little margin for success was unthinkable. A rare feeling inside her, Nell burst into the next room.

"Clydette, go out. Wait for LaBelle there."

The old slave-servant paralyzed. Never had the new family member acted like this.

"I do not listen to others' conversations, but I could not avoid hearing yours," Nell started harshly. She continued in a softer tone because LaBelle looked to be in shock. "If I am not mistaken you are advising Clydette to run away. You know how I feel. Never, never I had imagined you advocate such action. There are legal ways . . . " She stopped; these did exist but were equally almost impossible to obtain under any ownership.

"I am sorry, Master Miss Nell."

"Please, do not call me 'master'," Nell said, pacing. To take advantage of her privileged position was not in her nature. Besides, LaBelle was so frightened, unable to defend herself. "I am sure you want the best for Clydette, but that is not the right way," she said, looking straight at LaBelle without antagonism. The slave, head and eyes down seemed to have lost her vivacious spirit, willingness and ability to answer any statement, to find a way out of this illegal ground she had put herself on.

"I understand your intentions," Nell added, "but Clydette has a good future here. To jeopardize these benefits make no sense, LaBelle. Do you agree with me?"

"Yes, Miss Nell," she granted still looking down.

"Clydette will be fine. I will protect her; you know that," Nell continued now more confident that the matter would be resolved without further trouble. "Today it is very difficult to get freedom from your Master. The rumors of secession running around have complicated it, including your plans. This underground movement is very dangerous. Every plantation owner is aware of it and will punish anyone helping the escape of slaves."

LaBelle already knew this. She had been a slave for so many years and had witnessed countless obstacles on the road to freedom. She was aware very few who had ventured into that road, won liberty; others, death.

"Miss Nell, Clydette is so young. If she could go away what a difference her life would be!"

"LaBelle, escaping is almost impossible and you know it."

"Yes, Miss Nell. I just wanted a better life for her, if . . . " She stopped; crying, covered her face with both hands.

"I promise she will have the best as long as she is at my service," Nell consoled.

"I have no doubt, Miss Nell," she answered trying to control her emotions "It worries me if she is not."

"I see no reason why she should not be."

"Miss Nell, we never know what happens next."

"True, but if she continues helping you she will be familiar with the mansion, meaning she could be in charge when you can no longer do it," Nell prognosticated, giving to her words a strong tone capable of eliminating any doubt.

"Miss Nell, if things were as easy as you say . . . " LaBelle pointed out nodding.

"Where is the trouble?"

"Pardon, Miss Nell. You see, even I . . . not enough."

"I am afraid I do not understand."

"Miss Nell, I know you are right, but you cannot be with Clydette all the time."

"Of course not. Soon she will be a grown-up woman."

"You see, Miss Nell . . . there is the problem."

"I am teaching her manners and principles. If she follows them, she will do all right in life."

"I know, Miss Nell. I hope with all my heart it will be as you say and we will not regret it."

LaBelle pessimism filled Nell's patience. Shaking her head, she faced the weeping servant. "My goodness, why don't you believe me?"

"Miss Nell, I am afraid it could happen again," the old slave answered.

"For Christ, what are you talking about?"

LaBelle finally confessed her fear: "Rape."

"My God. If Clydette continues at the mansion, she will be more secure here than working in the cotton fields, right?"

"No, Miss Nell."

Nell was loosing patience. "LaBelle, why do you say that?"

The poor woman fidgeted. *Why did she have to ask?* LaBelle thought nervously. *Does she not know slaves have no rights at all for complaining about anything?* Nell observed the woman's discomfort. LaBelle realized that she had but one choice: to tell the whole story.

"Miss Nell, I should not say this but . . . the girl was raped inside the mansion."

"What?" an incredulous Nell shouted. "What girl?"

"The slave girl helping me who was killed by her boyfriend."

Slowly LaBelle's worries started to make sense. "Let us make it clear. Are you sure she was raped here?"

"Yes, Miss Nell."

A sudden anger came over Nell. How had such a thing happened under this roof without anybody noticing it? It seemed the frame of the building was thick enough to cover its secrets, but . . . "Are you certain, LaBelle?" she asked, still disbelieving.

"Yes, Miss Nell."

"How do you know it?"

"She told me."

"She had a boyfriend . . . "

"She broke up with him immediately after. She was too ashamed to tell him."

"Why did you not tell me . . . or Mr. Gilbert?"

"Nobody listens to us, Miss Nell. I did not want to bother you."

"I understand, I understand. Do you know who did it?" Nell ventured to ask, though frightened to hear the answer.

"Wade."

Nell looked seriously at the trembling woman. "Is that true, LaBelle?"

"She told me. When that happened, she did not come back. Her boyfriend tried to see her but she refused to receive him. When she knew she was pregnant, she wanted to run away. Then her boyfriend offered to help; they planned their escape, but it was not easy. They hid in the field. To reach the people of the underground movement takes time. Unfortunately, he was reported as a runaway slave to soon; they despaired, discussed it many times, and when nothing went right, they gave up hope of getting out. You know the rest: he killed her, attacked Wade, and hung himself. They had no other way . . . "

Now the picture of the situation was complete. LaBelle's behavior over the last weeks became clear and understandable and her desire to protect Clydette, justifiable. Only one actor of this drama had not been challenged so far. Nell did not like that.

Determined, with strong steps she went downstairs and entered her father-in-law's office. Her rapid movements immediately got Cecil's attention. Raising his eyes, he looked at Nell. It was very unusual for her to be there without announcing it first.

"Mr. Gilbert," she started, still unaccustomed to call him 'Father.'

"What is it? This must be important enough to interrupt my work," the gruff man said.

"I just heard something terrible," Nell said nervously, uncertain how the news would be received since she was still doubtful about her position within the family.

Cecil dropped the pen from his hand and calmly looked directly at her. Nell sat down in a chair in front of the big desk, breathing deeply and ordering the words in her mind, properly and precisely.

"The slain slave was raped," she said as quietly as possible, controlling her impulses as she let it out.

Cecil's face did not show surprise. Apparently, such a notice was not important enough. Something close to a grimace appeared on his face. "Nell, dear, that frequently happens," he said in a low but firm tone, pushing his body back from the desk. He was thinking, *This young woman . . . when is she going to grow?*

"Mr. Gilbert . . . it happened here." Nell saw a difference in his expression. Incredulity, perhaps?

"Nell, Nell you should not repeat everything you hear about these people."

"I am telling you she was raped in this mansion," she said, finally gathering the courage to speak clearly.

Cecil could not believe she was so naïve. Of course, that was an ingenuous idea.

"Dear . . . " He needed to bring down the ascendant tension visible in Nell's shivering hands. "Our house is sacred. We have kept it like that for a very long time and will continue to keep it the same way. Any slander will cause irreparable damage to our family's reputation." He stopped, giving her time to relax, to forget this displeasing suspicion. "I am certain you want to maintain it. This is your home, too. Therefore, do not spread false rumors, especially when they affect us."

He hoped he'd made his point clear and that this nonsense would end once and for all. But Nell shook her head. "My God! This is not gossip. Should I repeat it?"

This time for a second Cecil seemed disturbed. But he controlled himself. Leaning over the fancy desk he said, "Nell, dear, this is not the first occasion an unfounded accusation has been made, disappearing as fast as it came out." He looked firmly at his daughter-in-law. "Your information is inaccurate. This did not happen here."

"LaBelle would never say something so serious if it wasn't true," Nell responded, regretful that she'd had to reveal her source to confirm the veracity of her claim. Deep inside, she hoped that this would not cause headaches to the loyal server.

Cecil returned to a reposed position, thinking, trying to find the suitable, definitive words capable of stopping such ridiculous rumor.

"It was Wade." Nell, benefiting from a mute Cecil, put the decisive, final piece on the table. Cecil's facial expression had a slight change, although he kept quiet, figuring out how at least he could diminish the impact of this unpleasant revelation. It was evident that he wasn't going to be able to put the issue out of Nell's mind easily.

"This is upsetting," he said regaining aplomb and gazing around avoiding Nell's inquiring eyes.

"What are you going to do?" Nell asked.

"There is nothing *we* can do," Mr. Gilbert responded, making a gesture of impotency.

"Wade . . . will not be punished?" Nell asked incredulous.

"Dear, the woman is dead," Cecil reminded her.

Nell could not understand. What did her death have to do with punishing the rapist? She knew her next movement must be carefully crafted.

"That is true," she spoke slowly, searching for the clear, unquestionable reason capable of convincing Cecil of what she wanted. "Equally true is that Wade did not obey the instructions you surely gave him about this house, where you and your family live." She paused reviewing Cecil's reaction. Trusting her words had begun to break the hard armor that seemed to cover the master, Nell continued: "His action was a clear violation of your trust. He must be punished."

A long silence followed. Nell looked at her father-in-law wanting to penetrate his thoughts and discover how effective her arguments had been. She could guess very little. Cecil's face did not show any significant change, although now he looked somehow uneasy. Nell, today more experienced with his ways than she was during previous confrontations, simply waited, did not disturb his thinking.

"This matter will be cleared," Cecil promised realizing it was in his hands to end his son's wife's worries. "I will talk to Wade."

He looked at her with something close to a smile. The case ended. Closed. But not for Nell. She stayed there, waiting. Cecil could not believe she still had any concern. What else did she want? *If she were his wife . . .*

"I would like to know, besides scolding Wade, what you plan to do about the rape," she clarified for him.

For Cecil, this was going too far. Why was she so insistent about something that nobody could resolve?

"Dear, dear, that is now in the past. We cannot change it. Let it stay there."

"Are you saying . . . a man rapes a woman, no crime has been committed?"

"Nell, we keep our distance. Unfortunately, sometimes people do stupid things."

"And these 'stupid things,' as you called them, are not punishable?"

"In our community to accuse a white man of such an act is not advisable, Nell. The damage would be greater than any gain."

To continue arguing was useless, Nell sadly realized. The poor young woman. She felt a heavy burden over her body. Eyes to the ground, she kept immobile. Then, she stood up and walked toward the exit. Upon reaching the door, she turned to her father-in-law. Slowly, she firmly let him to know, "If I have any authority in this household, I wish to prohibit Wade for ever having anything to do with me."

Her voice and words were so clear that they left Cecil Gilbert speechless, amazed, as he watched her leaving.

Early the next day, Nell, as usual sat at the window in her apartment looking at Cecil's office. As customary, Wade came and walked into the office. Gabriel was not present; Cecil had sent him earlier to a nearby tobacco farm. Before going he told his father he agrees with his wife that Wade should be punished. During the long minutes Wade was in, Cecil's arguments were heard from the entrance hall to upstairs. When the foreman left, evidently he was mad. Afterward, Nell saw a familiar figure walking toward the private office. It was LaBelle. She knocked, pulled the door open and went inside. Nell's suspicion was confirmed when later LaBelle came out of the office shaking and in tears.

Life was not as usual at Gilbert's mansion. A rare sensation filled every room and person. Wade changed his daily meeting time. Nell hardly ever saw him. LaBelle was more reserved in spite of getting new assistants for the housework. Master Gilbert had ordered two older women from the fields to help in the mansion, releasing Clydette back to Nell's direct service.

LaBelle and her two helpers moved around inside the premises as one, always together; finishing one location, they moved to the next. Edna Gilbert stopped going to the small parlor after dinner; instead, retired straight to her apartments escorted by Anne, both missing the nightly family reunion. Nell was the only female present; therefore, she arranged to have a book there and sat apart, quietly reading and leaving the two men alone to discuss any subject, surely nothing of interest to her. Anyway, Cecil's cigar and smoke were getting into her nostrils too much.

It was shaping up to be another uneventful day when Nell heard angry shouting from downstairs, voice familiar but could not see who it was. She walked out her rooms; holding onto the balustrade to see the quarreling. There, at the entrance Wade was holding Clydette, shaking and yelling at her. The girl carrying a bag was trying to escape the man's grasp.

"Take off your dirty hands of her!" Nell ordered, running down the stairs. Wade, surprised, released the young woman. Reaching down, Nell took into her arms Clydette who was crying. As she started to guide the girl to go upstairs, Cecil came out of his office. Wade approached him.

"Mr. Gilbert, I saw the slave girl talking to that boy Anson."

The Master hesitated; looked at the two women going up the staircase. Recovering, he called, "Nell!"

She stopped halfway up, said a few words to Clydette and pushed her up before returning downstairs.

"I want to know," Cecil said, eyeing the slave girl and pointing up, "If she carries a letter." Anger was mounting higher on each word he pronounced.

"I sent her to pick up my order from Mr. Pierre," Nell explained, knowing she needed time to diffuse the storm that was evolving. Clydette, already upstairs, hid around the corner.

"Wade," Master Gilbert said to his employee, "are you certain?"

"Yes, Mr. Gilbert. I saw them talking."

Nell looked up the stairs; Clydette was now visible again. Nell ordered her to come down.

"Let's go inside the office," Cecil suggested. He opened the door, waving in Nell and Clydette, who was still carrying the bag. Then Cecil entered and closed the door after him, leaving Wade outside.

"Clydette, put the bag on the desk," Nell instructed her. "Mr. Gilbert, please check the items there."

The Master rapidly reviewed the contents of the bag, but he was not convinced when he found no letter. Therefore, rang the service bell calling for LaBelle. Soon, the loyal servant walked into the office. Cecil Gilbert ordered her to search Clydette. Nell kept quiet while the servant fulfilled the Master's orders. No letter was found. Mr. Gilbert was still somehow skeptical. He knew Wade was not completely trustworthy but it was unlikely he would lie in a matter like this. Even so, Cecil did not question Clydette. If she denies it, he could not use pressure. Nell's presence voided any radical method. Later he would look after and give strict orders to the loyal slave but for now he allowed the three women to leave.

Nell was relieved the incident ended well. She told Anne she was walking on risky, perilous ground and that another method must be used. If Clydette was discovered carrying messages, it would bring terrible consequences to the young slave. Anne, however, secure of a brilliant future, was too happy for worries. Anson had renewed his promises, assurances of overcoming all obstacles. Since he was learning a new trade, he would advance enough to be able to formally request her hand in matrimony.

Next day Gabriel was ready to leave Cecil's office after updating him on the daily chores. "Son," his father stopped him, "while in Roseville drop by M. Pierre's boutique. Check if that boy Anson is still working there."

"Why?"

"Nothing important. Simple curiosity."

"Is there any problem, Father?"

"No," the man said in a light tone.

But Gabriel knew him too well. That attitude meant something. "Is this related to Anne?" he pressed. Mr. Cecil Gilbert shook his head, keeping his eyes on the papers on his desk. "To continue trying to discourage Anne may do the opposite," Gabriel said slowly, facing the apparently serene man. "She is not a child, left her alone. She finally will realize who he is and will reject any pretension he may have."

"Nobody can guarantee that," Cecil affirmed looking straight at his son. "Problems must be taken care of at first sight. Anyway, I will never consent my daughter to relate with somebody coming from an underprivileged family."

Gabriel could argue against this thinking; however, loyalty and respect prevented him.

"You wanted to see me, Mr. Gilbert?" Nell asked, entering the office. The Master, signaling a chair, invited her to sit. Leaning over the papers scattered over the bureau, Cecil dropped the question: "Did Anne receive letters recently?" There was no emotion or special interest in his tone; he looked up and focused his gaze on her face.

"You are asking the wrong person," Nell answered, withstanding the firm scrutiny of his eyes.

"I do not think so," Cecil said, resting back in the executive chair. "The information I have points directly at you."

"You have been misinformed."

"Nell, Nell, we are grown-ups. Let us not play games. Did she . . . ?"

"I already answered you."

"Your husband confirmed this boy does not work at M. Pierre's business. They have seen him at the pharmacy delivering orders." Cecil used his friendliest tone to disclose his knowledge about the case, pretending no displeasure. "Wade had seen him talking to Clydette. He possibly gave her letters for Anne. I am asking you once more: is this information correct?"

Nell stayed firm. "Again, I am the wrong person. The last time I saw him was long ago at the county fair."

Master Gilbert breathed heavily. "Nell, my patience has a limit," he said. "You and Anne are close; you must know what is going on. What do you talk about in the garden?"

"We read educational materials and scientific books. She is completing her education," Nell answered coldly.

"Has this Anson ever come while you are there?"

"Of course not!"

"How often has Anne received letters?" Cecil asked rapidly, trying to catch her off guard.

"That is a private matter only Anne can answer."

Cecil realized could not break Nell's resistance, loyalty to her principles. He rested his arms on the desk. "I had hoped to get help from my daughter-in-law. I am disappointed."

"Mr. Gilbert, I will never betray someone's confidence," Nell responded calmly. The meeting ended.

The next day Nell saw Anne going into her father's office. *Bad sign*, she thought. Instantly she knew why Anne had been called down. Nell anxiously waited, glancing downstairs frequently as she paced her apartment. After a short time, Anne came out crying and went up to her rooms. Nell wanted to console her, but out of respect to her father-in-law, she abstained to go.

Going downstairs Nell held her steps; Darlene was entering the mansion. Almost running the guest went directly to Edna's place. Nell waited till she got there, and then came down the rest of the way. From the half-opened door of Edna's apartment, Nell heard Darlene's faltering, excited voice: "I have it! . . . Gabriel's mistress . . . her name is Vilma Mullen!"

Without hesitation, Nell opened wide the door and walked into Edna's room. The two women froze.

"What did you say?" Nell firmly asked walking toward Darlene.

"Nell," Edna said advancing to her, "somebody who just moved to Roseville. We don't know who she is; that's correct, Darlene?"

But the informer was too afraid and not really interested in denying it; her head lowered, avoiding both women's eyes. Nell kept facing Darlene. The visitor knew she had no escape: "Her name is . . . Vilma Mul . . . " she nervously repeated.

Nell left the room in haste. Edna wished to say a word to lighten the news but she had no time. Both women came to the door and saw Nell climbing the stairs in a hurry.

"LaBelle!" Nell called before reaching her apartment.

From a downstairs room, the servant came out. Edna directed her upstairs. Rapidly, LaBelle went up. Nell ordered her to find and bring Gabriel home immediately. By the time the young man arrived a while later, Darlene had gone. Edna, too disgusted, locked her apartment's door.

"Love, what happened?" the man asked his wife.

"Nothing important. I just heard you have a mistress."

The news hit him badly. All his strength left his body. He opened his mouth but he could not make a sound. Nell, moving fast in front of him, shaking, and weeping profusely overrode any energy he could muster to think or say anything.

"How could you do this to me? Betraying my trust!" She turned her back going to the end of the room. "I completely believed . . . put my confidence in you . . . and this is how you regard me? With a mistress!" She came back, avoiding looking at him.

"Nell, please . . . " Pulling all the will he could gather to recuperate, finally words came out: "It is not . . . "

"No, Mr. Gilbert?" she reposted defiantly. "Can you say there is no lover?"

No matter how hard he tried, Gabriel could not conjure a word or explanation that could counter her clear, irrefutable accusation.

"I do not want you in my bedroom." Nell went back to the end of the room. "I will ask LaBelle to arrange the parlor for you to sleep there, and from now on, we will speak only the strictly necessary."

Bluntly, she laid out her conditions; turning dried her cheeks with her hands and firmly looked at him. The sight disturbed her: she never had seen such sorrowful face. If she had been aware of it, she might have used another tone, or softer words. For reasons she didn't know in this sad hour, Gabriel's face, contracted, full of tears, indicated that he was hurt very hard.

"WAR . . .! WAR . . .!" Loud yelling came from downstairs. Gabriel and Nell rushed to the hall overlooking the main entrance.

"We are at the war!" Down there was Dexter. Running around excited, smiling, very happy, his hair disheveled, he kept announcing the news that many people feared and others welcomed. "We seceded! The Union is broken. A new government was established in Montgomery!" Dexter continued informing walking up and down the large foyer, repeating again and again the events just had occurred.

Cecil came out of his office, Edna from her apartment, watching the young man incredulously. Nell observed the scene. The Master did not seem much in agreement with the excitement shown by Dexter. Did the young man really realize the seriousness of the news? In any case, Nell was in no mood for anything, so she went back to her place. Anne came out of her apartment and joined Gabriel going downstairs, compelled by the euphoria Dexter displayed.

"War! We are at war! Dixie . . . *long live Dixie!*"

Dixie

After that day nothing was as in the past. The coming and going of people made the mansion look like a garrison. News of secession was the main subject for those with large number of slaves. Organizing militias and vigilant groups inside each plantation and keeping out the religious men believed to be responsible for spreading the idea of liberty between the slaves were at the forefront of every owner's mind.

Gabriel and Nell's separation did not cause great commotion; war relegated it to a lower position. Nevertheless, it was not a secret that Gabriel was greatly affected. Cecil suggested exercising his authority to make her to change her attitude. Gabriel pointed out that Nell was a Northern woman with principles far different from those of the South. When Cecil insisted Gabriel reminded his father that he, too, was unable to overcome his mother's decision to live apart. Cecil, against his will, did not persist.

Aunt Mabel came to visit Nell. After the salutations, they sat in the bedroom; the small parlor at the entrance to the apartment was now Gabriel's territory. The conversation started with the main theme of the day, war and the women agreed that terrible days were to follow.

Soon after, Aunt Mabel looking straight at Nell, with tears coming to her eyes, said, "Nell, I do not intervene into the private lives of others but Gabriel is suffering."

Nell crossed her arms sternly. "Sorry, Aunt Mabel; he provoked this situation."

"Yes, Nell and are not both of you in pain?"

"I never wanted to cause harm to anyone and I did nothing to deserve it."

"I know, I know, Nell dear. But you must talk."

"Nothing justifies his action," Nell answered firmly.

"That is true, but we should listen to everybody," good Aunt Mabel pointed out calmly with her sweet voice.

Nell replied, "I know you love him and will do anything in his favor but right now I am very disappointed and cannot overcome my disillusionment."

"I understand, dear. Probably my Gabriel fell into this without realizing its consequences."

"Certainly nobody obligated him."

"You are right again, dear. Poor Gabriel . . . he made a big mistake following the crowd."

Nell looked at her. "What crowd?"

"Yes, Nell, in this society most of these 'gentlemen' have a paramour. Remember the woman staring at us during our first visit to Roseville? Her name is Flora Hobson . . . Cecil's mistress."

"What?" That was news for Nell. Standing up, she walked around shaking her head. Had she heard correctly? Upright Cecil Gilbert has a lover?

"Yes, dear. That's why Edna separated."

"I always had some reservation with him," Nell said, "but it never crossed my mind he was . . . "

Aunt Mabel nodded her head slowly. "We human beings are very peculiar."

Nell sat again, still perplexed.

"Surely this answers many questions about them," the good Aunt continued.

"Aunt Mabel, this is so unthinkable that I am completely lost."

"Well, dear, we all make mistakes."

"How long have Edna and her husband been living apart?"

"I would say since Anne celebrated her first birthday."

"Then, they lived together a long time. Anne is much younger than her brother."

"Nell, Anne was born after Edna and Cecil reconciled once, when Flora disappeared from Roseville. Then, suddenly, she came back. This time, Edna never forgave her husband, assumed a lower position in the family affairs as you have already noticed."

"That explains many things. But why did Edna not leave him?"

"No place to go. She is from Charleston, as Cecil. Her only living relative, my husband, was Cecil's partner and living here."

"I did not know they came from that city. Why did they move?"

"Nell, dear, it is a long story."

"I have time; if you want, my ears are ready."

Aunt Mabel seemed undecided, not certain if it was appropriate to tell her. Nell kept quiet, waiting. Anyway, Aunt Mabel reasoned, it was better to tell Nell since her version would be closer to what happened than anyone else's.

"Years ago when Cecil was young, an accountant firm employed him as a messenger. Cecil stayed after work often, studying and teaching himself the business. Therefore, he was later promoted. Soon after, he married Edna."

Aunt Mabel stopped gazing at Nell. Then she continued: "The office was on the second floor; the first was occupied by a bank. Cecil always worked till late at night, and his reputation as a hard worker was recognized. One day, the bank discovered funds were missing. Special agents came to help when the local authorities could not find who was culpable, how the money had disappeared. They concluded that someone had illegally entered the bank when part of the ceiling of a back room showed that recently was removed and no repair in that place was performed by the bank. A visual inspection of the second floor of the building by specialists was planned for the following days. But one night, fire damaged the second level. The accounting office was almost destroyed. Rumors circulated that Cecil was seen that night in the building. Later, when arrested, he hired the best lawyers in Charleston. The bank offered a substantial reward to anyone with information on the robbery but nobody appeared to testify at the trial. Cecil was found not guilty due to insufficient proofs and released. For the next months neither he nor Edna were seen; they retired from public view. Months later he opened an accounting business but his name damaged, nobody used his services."

"By now, Gabriel was born. Cecil decided to leave the city; no future there. He traveled searching for a friendlier place, going so far as New Orleans. I forgot to mention Cecil appeared to be wealthy now. Money was no a problem; Edna had new clothing and servants. Finally, I don't know why or how he chose Roseville, but here is where they settled. When my husband accepted to work for Cecil, we moved too." Aunt Mabel stopped, relaxing for some time. Then, she continued:

"The Gilberts' mansion surprised us; Cecil had bought a plantation and slaves. Life was perfect. Cecil treated my husband very generously who supervised everything but bookkeeping, he was in charge of that and this is all I know." Aunt Mabel ended apologizing: "Nell, dear, I'm sorry if I talk too much. You haven't said a word . . . "

"That's fine, Aunt Mabel. Thanks for telling me. Does Gabriel know this?"

"Probably not. He was too little; besides, Cecil and Edna never mentioned anything about living in Charleston." Aunt Mabel waited for Nell to comment, but she said nothing. Speechless, she remained deep in her thoughts. Aunt Mabel respected her silence. Later, she said: "My dear, I must go. What will you do with poor Gabriel?"

Nell stood and faced her. "I need to get my thoughts and feelings back, in right order," she answered slowly. "Sorry if he is suffering . . . did he send you?"

"No; we just talked. He did tell me he never visited that woman after you came," Aunt Mabel said going to the door. She added, "Remember, I am always available, if you need anything." With that, they said good-by and she left.

Cecil dismissed Wade from news briefing. Instinctively, he looked out the window, viewing the entrance trail. A woman carrying an umbrella was entering the path toward the mansion.

"*Wade!*" he shouted causing the employee who had almost reached the front door, to freeze. Running, he came back to the office.

"Stop her!" Cecil ordered visibly upset as he pointed to the outside road. "That woman cannot come into this house."

Wade did not wait for second instructions; rapidly, he left. Nell heard Cecil's loud voice. She went to the window overlooking downstairs and saw Wade leaving in a hurry. She rushed back to the bedroom and to the window facing the entrance to the mansion. Down there, Wade was reaching a woman walking in. Stepping in front, he halted her steps; holding her arm he forced her to turn back.

The woman was Vilma, that's certain, Nell guessed. She couldn't be sure since the view from upstairs was blocked by the umbrella covering the woman's head. But who else could the visitor be? Nell retired from the window, somehow happy that Wade was so efficient in carrying out the Master's orders. Right now she had no desire to meet with an old girlfriend.

Life now unfolded according to news from the belligerent war zone. States were seceding, a new President installed, the Southern Confederacy was established and battles won and lost. Therefore, enthusiasm rule one day and sorrow the next, lowering everyone's hopes. Even so, the regional patriotic sentiment was always high.

Dexter came to the mansion wearing a Confederate uniform. Cecil and Gabriel received him, surprised and worried. Gabriel did not seem to agree completely with his decision to joining up. The army so far had numerous volunteers and someone with Dexter's social position was not likely nowadays to take a military career. Anyway, they congratulated, embraced and wished him many victories in Southern battles.

Nell and Anne came down and joined Edna saluting him with warm desires for success in his new adventure.

"We are leaving today," Dexter informed them. "There is a farewell parade in town this afternoon."

"I'll be there," Gabriel promised.

"Me too," Anne joined.

Some hours after, Gabriel opened the door of Cecil's private office. Wade was there, talking to Cecil. As soon as Gabriel walked in, Wade stopped talking and stepped away. "Mister Gabriel, the coach is outside," Wade said.

"I am waiting for Anne."

Moments later, Anne came into the office along with Nell whose presence surprised Gabriel. "We are ready," Anne told her brother.

"Anne," Cecil said standing up and coming to the group, "I do not think you should go."

"Why not, Father?" she asked annoyed.

Cecil came back to the desk. Turning, he faced his daughter. "A young lady has no place there."

"Father, everyone will be watching the soldiers going out of town. I don't . . . "

"Listen, Anne. Your mother does not feel well. You must take care of her."

"She was fine, I saw her not long ago," Anne responded.

"That was before. You must stay with your mother," Cecil ordered firmly.

Anne wanted to go. It had been a long time since she had seen other people. But knowing her father, any argument against him would be futile. Nell, now more experienced with how things were around here, did not speak; her position in the family was already damaged and to worsen it would not be wise.

"Of course, Nell can go," The Master granted.

Did I ask for permission? Nell thought indignantly. But her words were milder. "I was going to accompany Anne. If she is not allowed, I will not go either."

Cecil looked at Nell, thinking she was trying to strong-arm him into letting Anne take the trip, as well. *Who gave her that authoritarian attitude?* Yet, he restrained from making a comment. *She should do as Gabriel commands; she is his wife!* was his next thought.

But Gabriel did not interfere. He could not argue with his father and he had already lost his wife's confidence; there was nothing he could do. Anne left the room annoyed, followed by Nell.

Wade stopped the carriage at a good spot in town. A huge multitude occupied the plank sidewalks. Dexter's parents along with Darlene and her family were at M. Pierre's boutique front door. The military parade started soon. Young men on horses opened the event under the enthusiastic onlookers' applause. Dexter, riding a magnificent equine was promptly recognized and received warm salutations as he rode by, happy and proud. Gabriel, standing in the coachman's seat, waved his arms at his friend who smiling returned the affection from family, friends and neighbors. A strange feeling constricted Gabriel's chest as the dust blocked the leaving cavalcade.

Next, soldiers on foot marching along the main road received equal roar approval and farewell exclamations. Children ran along their sides, hardly holding their emotions, some calling those passing by their names.

A young soldier in the parade got Gabriel's attention. It was Anson. Then, he was going away, to different places that held countless dangers and many tempting new opportunities. So, Anson *may* forget Anne. That would change many things.

Coming back to reality, Gabriel paid attention to the next attraction, an open carriage with side signs reading: VOLUNTEER

NURSES. The wagon surprised everyone. Smiling young women rode in the vehicle, satisfied with the unanimous approval of the excited citizens cheering them. As the wagon got closer, Gabriel recognized one volunteer: Vilma Mullen. Never crossed his mind she would join the war effort. Gabriel sat on the coach seat. She is going out of town. Could that help to find a possible solution to his marital problem?

Nell approached the main entrance of the mansion followed by Anne and Clydette, playing with a ball. These afternoons they had resumed meeting in the gardens at Anne's request. At same time, Wade arrived on his horse and dismounting, he opened the door and let the women pass first. "Miss, a letter from Boston," Wade said courteously, handing Nell an envelope from others he was carrying (he knew due the letter was from her family, he could break Nell's orders). She took it, noticing in Wade's hands another wrinkled envelope with Anne's name on it. Nell walked into the house, followed by Anne and Clydette, going to the staircase. Wade came in last and walked straight to Cecil's office.

"Nell, you got mail"

"Yes, Anne. I believe you too."

"Really, Nell?"

"Your name was on an envelope Wade was holding."

Grabbing Nell by an arm, Anne stopped; anxiety on her face. Only one person would write to her. "Nell, come with me."

They went back down the stairs, Nell putting her letter in a pocket for the time being as they went straight to the private office. Anne knocked at the door and she opened it. Cecil looked at them and dismissed Wade hurriedly.

"Did I receive a letter?" Anne asked. Caught with his guard down, Cecil did not respond; instead covered with his hands the papers on his desk.

Cecil looked at the couple; he did not believe it. Finally, he said, "If you have mail, it will be delivered."

That was a Cecil's typical solution, to play dumb. Anne knew it. She also was aware that if she did not get it now, never will.

"Nell saw an envelope addressed to me," Anne boldly informed him. "I want it, Father."

How could she say that? Suddenly she was no longer afraid. Cecil's eyes darted from one side to the other. *What's going on? When did I lose control?* He decided he needed to play strong. "Have you forgotten who I am? How *dare* you talk to me like this?" he thundered.

"I just want what belongs to me," Anne insisted.

"Is disobedience what you have been learning lately?" the man shot angrily, hardly holding his composure. Changing his gaze to Nell, he asked, "Is this what you are doing, turning my daughter against me, making a rebel of her?"

"That's not true, Mr. Gilbert," Nell promptly defended herself.

"I am responsible of my attitude," Anne declared. "Nell always has told me the straight thing," she added to reaffirm her words.

Cecil sensed a strong alliance between them. "This is not the fact we are witnessing," he said visibly disturbed.

"If there is a letter I want it," Anne demanded.

"I am your father. I know what is best for you."

"I am not a child; I can make my own decisions!"

Cecil sighed. Clearly he had no choice. He slowly shuffled a few papers around on his desk, pulled a long, squeezed envelope out, and handed it to Anne. The two women walked toward the door.

"You must be satisfied, Nell," Cecil blamed her; a tone in his voice that they had never heard. It was impotence. He needed to get this burning fire off of his chest. "My daughter is against me; my son is unhappy. You should have given me a grandson; instead, you brought discord, rebellion . . . "

Nell froze. Those words hurt her. To cause trouble was far from her intentions. "The only one responsible for your troubles, Mr. Gilbert, is your intransigence."

Anne, aware of the critical situation, forced Nell to keep moving, leaving the office.

Once alone in her apartment, Nell opened the letter she had received. Soon, sorrow came to her face; the news from Boston, not good. Her father was sick and the attending doctor had been unable to clearly diagnose the illness affecting him. He had improved lately but only partially. Now he was resting at home.

Nell walked around, thinking, analyzing the prevailing situation. She wanted to go back to Boston but the precarious political situation plus her marriage problem would make it more difficult. Nell sat on a chair, needing to organize her thoughts. First, she would talk to Gabriel. He must help if she was to overcome any opposition from Cecil.

"Nell! Nell!" Anne came running, excited. She knelt in front of her sister-in-law. "I am the happiest woman in the world!" Showing her a piece of paper Anne continued, "Anson loves me; he promises to marry and take care of me for the rest of his life!"

"Oh, my God, Anne!"

"Nell, he asked me to wait for him; he says he will do whatever is necessary to come back soon and ask my father for my hand in matrimony."

"I am so happy, Anne!" With an effusive embrace she congratulated the thrilled young woman.

"I knew the letter was from him. That is why I insisted so much," Anne said.

"Thanks God Mr. Gilbert gave it to you."

"Yes, Nell. I was surprised he did. I must watch the mail very closely. Anson said he will write frequently. I do not want to miss any letter."

"I promise to keep an eye on the mail, Anne."

"Thank you, Nell. I knew you would help me."

"And where is Anson now?" Nell questioned.

"He cannot mention the city or place but so far, he is happy," Anne replied.

"That is understandable."

Anne was moved, hopeful. "When Anson comes back from fighting, Father will have no valid arguments to reject him."

Nell agreed with her, supporting the marvelous spirit of love the young lady was experiencing. At the same time, she knew that Cecil's opinion would dictate the coming events. Today the world was full of uncertainties. A war going on indicated caution and recommended prudence. But Nell did not give any cautionary advice; she let Anne's dreams fly without the shadow of a doubt. For now, she mentioned the bad news received.

Before dinner that evening, Cecil was informed that Edna was not feeling well and was staying in her chambers. Nell told Gabriel the letter received about her father and asked for his help. He promised that he would do his best. Downstairs in the dining room, LaBelle served the meal and then left to bring Edna a dish she had prepared specially for her.

Gabriel started the conversation. "Father, Mr. Dumont is ill. Nell wishes to travel to Boston."

"Son," Cecil answered eyes on the table, "that is dangerous these days. Since she needs to, must go by the safest, securest possible route."

"Thank you, Mr. Gilbert," Nell gratefully acknowledged her father-in-law's rapid consent. With that, the subject was no longer discussed. After dinner, Anne and Nell went to see Edna. Cecil and Gabriel stayed downstairs for their nightly meeting.

"Nell, when will you be back?" Later Anne asked on their way upstairs.

Though appropriate and timely, the query seemed unanswerable. Only the bad news of her father's illness had occupied Nell's attention. She had not even thought of a returning date.

"Please, Nell, tell me when you are coming back," Anne begged, extremely anxious. Upon reaching the upper level, they stopped. At this time Nell was unable to even think about tomorrow. Moving South had helped to consolidate her maturity but tears now covering Nell's eyes and nervousness blocked any sensible thought. Genuine affection had developed between her and Anne. In an emotional impulse, they embraced, both trembling.

"I do not know, Anne. It depends on too many things . . . "

"I will miss you so much!"

Even though Nell knew this was true, she could not promise, predict the unfolding of coming events.

The news from the armed conflict was sporadic and many now positive, propitiated Nell's travel arrangements. Gabriel checked all possible connections in order to get a direct, safe route for Nell. Clydette, first thought to be a traveling companion, was eliminated since black people going north were suspicious of treachery. Therefore, Nell had to travel alone. She was trusted to handle the situation.

When the departure day arrived, Gabriel drove the carriage to the train station. He made sure the luggage was taken care of and Nell's reserved compartment was comfortable and secure. When it was time to leave, Gabriel showing a revolver, asked her to carry it. She rejected it, had never used one. But due to the volatile situation, he insisted, begged her. To avoid discussing in public, Nell accepted. Gabriel gave her quick instructions about the gun's use. She put it into her purse.

Extending a hand in a polite gesture, Nell looked at her husband. Tears began running down Gabriel cheeks, giving Nell an uncomfortable feeling. Rapidly she turned and went inside the coach and walked into the coach compartment. Gabriel watched the cars moving down the station. Nell avoided sitting near the window; she did not want him to see tears in her eyes.

Later, into the journey, Nell put aside the book. She turned her eyes to the window to watch the countryside, wild forest, bushes and the country familiar scenery. The rid evoked memories of the great lifting sensation she had received when coming from Boston, when she first saw the exuberant Southern wilderness. For some time, the view did not change; the trees were not as corpulent as she remembered. *Maybe due to the season*, she thought. She tried to continue reading. Later, she checked her watch; soon it would be dinnertime. She laid the book aside and began to look the landscape again. The view shook her. What was that? Desolate, barren fields extending to the horizon. *For goodness sake, what happened?* she wondered, amazed. Where the splendid forest, the wild, beautiful flowers, the copious vegetation that not long ago covered these lands? A sad, bitter sentiment ran from head to toes. How could this be possible, such devastating damage to this fertile soil? *War, Nell*, she said to herself. *The evil of men at work.*

Early next day, the train stopped outside of a small, crowded town near some old, rustic huts, probably slaves' dwellings. There was activity all around. Confederate soldiers and other people going in a hurry everywhere. Trouble was in the air.

Nell caught a glimpse of a black man, well-dressed compared with others around, walking along the railroad tracks talking to an old black woman. She suddenly walked to the other side of the road and disappeared into the crowd. The black man came toward the railroad; his figure was familiar. Then Nell recognized him: it was John Smith, her father's messenger. She opened the coach window; drawing out her head, she called him.

The man froze. He seemed more afraid than anything else. Following the voice, he looked at the train. Nell, waving both arms, made herself visible. He came closer to the wagon.

"Miss Nell, what a surprise."

"I'm so glad to see somebody I know."

"What a coincidence to meet you here," John said, looking around.

"I'm going back home. I received news my father is not well."

"Yes, Miss. I heard he's sick."

"Do you know anything? My mother did not say much."

"Sorry, Miss, I left soon after hearing the news."

"What are you doing down here?" asked Nell.

"Traveling on personal business, Miss Dumont."

"Do you know why the train stopped here?"

People were coming and going near the train in a rush, some special activity had happened nearby. John checked at both directions under the curious look of people passing by, wondering why a black man was talking to a white lady. The looks made him uneasy.

"Don't know. Sorry, I must leave; have a pleasant trip." He left, almost running. Nell had no time to say anything. She lost sight of him immediately. John seemed not to be in a hurry but wanting to hide.

The sound of marching soldiers mixed with noisy traffic distracted Nell's attention. A cavalry unit troop appeared coming straight to the train. When they got closer, she could see their tired faces that gave her a somber feeling. Many of them showed dirty uniforms. She went back inside the compartment.

The marching men stopped at the train. An officer dismounting came to the cars followed by soldiers. Nell watched them to climb aboard. She sat wondering about their presence. Moments later a knock at the door interrupted her thoughts; it was an attendant, who informed her presence was requested in the luggage car by the military. Nell picked up her purse and followed the employee's instructions to the required location. There, other ladies and gentlemen already gathered. The officer Nell had seen outside was directing soldiers checking opened trunks. Later, he asked Nell to identify her luggage. Nell advanced toward the piled, scattered units on the floor and pointed out three of them.

"Please, I need to inspect them," the officer requested.

Nell took the keys from her purse and handed them to the soldier standing by. He opened the trunks, checking inside. "Miss, where are you traveling to?" the officer questioned.

"Boston," replied Nell.

"Long trip," he said.

"Due to military operations near places this train will pass, there is a delay for passenger security," the officer explained, addressing the people there. That answered many of Nell's questions. "The luggage will be transferred to another car of the convoy. The army needs this one," the officer informed.

Inconveniences due the prevailing war situation were common and complaints useless. Therefore, nobody disputed the orders.

"Does anyone have any idea how long the train will stay here?" Nell asked, breaking the silence.

"If no new perilous conditions arise, it will leave late tomorrow," the officer answered.

One by one, the passengers left the luggage wagon to their respective seats, accepting the hazards the special circumstances of fighting a war placed on their lives. Nell went back to her compartment. This was becoming a memorable journey.

Nell had dinner early to avoid the crowds in the dining coach. She was, as many, not in a good mood. Back in her compartment, she did the only thing available which was to gaze outside. The view remained the same: pedestrians and soldiers coming and going. As night approached, more soldiers were seen; this time, injured ones being helped by nurses, young men on stretchers walking painfully, some helped, others alone. The endless parade of wounded could disturb even the most indifferent soul.

Nell realized the officer had told the truth; nearby combat had taken place. The amount of injured men clearly demonstrated that casualties had been heavy. As the number of soldiers coming grew, any hope of departing soon, dimmer. To see young boys wounded, away from their families, fighting a war with more pride than resources and with no end in sight, was depressing. Right now leaving the South was a wise decision, she told herself. A knock at the door stopped her thoughts. She rushed to open it, hoping it was good news. At the entrance was a nurse. Recognizing her was shocking, paralyzed Nell. It was Vilma Mullen.

"We need to talk," the unexpected visitor said firmly.

"We have nothing to discuss," Nell riposted. Her first impulse to shut the door was stopped by the rapid movement of Vilma stepping into the room. Nell had no choice but to walk toward the end of the cabin, facing the window. Vilma closed the door. Patiently, she waited giving Nell time to relax and accept the challenge; there was no place to hide. Nell sat; bad moments, better to handle immediately than to ignore them.

"I want to say," Vilma started with soft, clear voice, "everything I will tell you is true. I need not to lie."

She stopped breathing deeply, visibly holding back emotions. "I came to Roseville before and without knowing Gabriel was getting married. He only came to provide the necessary things for my subsistence when his employees could not." She paused again, resting, gaining strength. Then continued: "He asked me to leave. I promised I would but I had no place to go. The only city I knew, Boston had too recent bad memories for me. I know now I did wrong. I should have left Roseville immediately, but for the first time in a long, long period, I had finally found peace.

And more importantly, it never crossed my mind that I might be hurting anyone. That certainly was not my intention." As Vilma finished, she was looking down, her face appearing more tranquil. Nell, with many new thoughts, stayed quiet; she always had been a good listener.

"I can assure he never was untrue to you. I tried to speak with you but was not allowed into the mansion. I just wanted to tell Gabriel . . . Mr. Gilbert loves you very much. He is emotionally paying hard for this mistake. Again, it happened before, not after your wedding . . . " Nearly crying, Vilma trailed off.

Nell, eyes down, did not speak. To hear another version of the events that had shattered her life was convenient. Now she had new material to analyze and perhaps, she should reconsider the actions she had taken.

Vilma spoke again. "Becoming a nurse gave me the opportunity to begin a new life. I will never return to Roseville," she promised. Slowly, she turned and opened the door. "I wish the best life can bestow you," she said going out.

Nell raised her head. She had no time to say anything. Vilma was gone. Nell turned to the window and saw people rushing, helping injured soldiers and going about pressing business. There were many nurses, but not a sight of Vilma. She had disappeared as quickly as she had come.

Nell sat. How had Vilma known she was there? She probably saw her through the window and had the courage to come and talk to her. The high, friendly opinion of Vilma at least in part, was restored. After all, Vilma had a history of good behavior which could not be achieved by a fake or duplicitous person. After a few moments of reflection, Nell had a new sentiment of acknowledgment toward Gabriel and Vilma's relationship. It was something to think about later. For now the road she was on must be completed. She could not have peace of mind till reaching home and seeing her sick father.

The door suddenly opened. At the entrance stood a tall, dirty, bearded soldier, his hair in disarray. Rapidly he came in, closing the door.

"Ah, what I found!" the malicious intruder said. "Have money or jewelry, perhaps?"

Nell controlled her initial nervous tremor; not time to panic. "Certainly, sir," she answered bringing a faked smile to her face. "I have a collar." She grabbed her purse and searched inside. "Here it is."

The face of the man, surely a deserter, changed dramatically: she was aiming a gun at him.

"I know how to use it," the defiant woman said, and to prove it she released the security lock fast and precisely.

The man raised his arms, signaling surrender. "Easy, lady . . . easy!" he begged. Slowly stepping back, he opened the door and left as fast as he had entered.

Nell breathed deeply, thanking God Gabriel had insisted on carrying the revolver and she had the nerves to use it. *How did that man get in?* Nell pondered. Oh, yes. When Vilma left, she did not lock the door inside. She would have to be more careful.

After the mentally exhausting day, Nell could not sleep. The activity outside on the railroad track never stopped. She took a book and tried to read. A few chapters later, it became more peaceful outside. She put the book down, said her prayers, and fell asleep. The rest of the night was quiet as gradually, normalcy at last seemed to come back to the small railroad town.

Nell woke up, it was still dark. She got dressed anyway, thinking it is better to be ready for the next contingency. While brushing her hair, she heard noise outside the compartment. Remembering the previous incident, she cautiously went to the door. She could make out the sound of people outside pushing a heavy object along the floor.

"Who is there?"

Instantly, the noise stopped, but the presence of somebody was certain. "Answer me or I will pull the alarm bell," Nell warned.

"Miss Nell," a soft voice replied, "please . . ."

"Who are you?"

"John, Miss . . . John Smith."

Nell opened the door. In the hall was John, his face worried, and a young black man and a woman, shaking. A big, heavy trunk was on the floor.

"Miss Nell, I am sorry to disturb you. I am traveling on this train too," John explained, glancing at his visibly frightened companions.

"My God, we see again," Nell said.

"These young people are helping me with my trunk. It is heavy . . . "

Nell looked at them. Why was the young black couple so nervous? Anyway, it was not her business. "Are you going back to Boston?" Nell questioned.

"No, Miss. Not yet," John responded.

"Well, I'll see you later, since you are coming on this train," she said closing the door.

A short while later, Nell went out; she needed to go to the luggage coach to pick up clothing. She walked the narrow hall through the next car; the passengers still sleeping. She pulled the door which opened slowly, stepping into the new luggage compartment, trunks piled tight. There, at a corner she saw John closing the cover of his trunk over the young black couples' heads, forcing them down.

"Bend your knees more," John instructed them.

"For goodness sake, John! What are you doing?"

"Miss Nell," John walked to her, excited. "Please, leave and say nothing."

The black couple stood up in the open trunk. Shaking, they embraced. "Ma'am," the young man said, looking at Nell. "Lemme . . . I'm . . . diz bizness fer my fambly . . . " he stuttered, emotions high.

"Please," Nell interrupted him, aware how afraid he was with her presence. "I will not say a word, promised."

"I know she will not," John supported her, bringing relief to the young couple. "I need to think. I must get you out of here."

John asked the couple to get inside the trunk again, placing their legs and arms in different positions. But when he put the cover down, still did not close properly.

"John, there is no way they will fit in there," Nell told him.

"They must go; it is too late, they cannot go back," John said.

"Take one of my suitcases," Nell suggested.

John looked at her. The idea was too risky. He rejected it.

"There is no other solution," Nell affirmed. John knew she was right. Soon, the sun would come up and the bustle of people would begin again. There was no time to find a better solution. Rapidly, Nell went through the different pieces of luggage until finding hers. One big enough was half-emptied, transferring the clothing to John's trunk. The new container was ample enough for the young couple.

Back in her compartment, Nell remembered LaBelle promoting Clydette's run away, how strongly she opposed her and tonight she had helped two slaves to escape lured by the perilous but worthy road to freedom.

That morning at breakfast, Nell asked the waiter for any news about departing. So far, nothing. However, the military movements were decreasing, a promising signal, he assured. Back in her compartment Nell scanned the outside. The traffic was normal though there were still a few soldiers and nurses. Afterward, an attendant came informing her that the train would be leaving soon. That was the best announcement she had heard in a long time.

Soon the train recovered its life. People were coming on board, passing through, and talking. At last the voyage will continue. Nell would miss the view; she'd never forget this town. The engine started up, steam coming out, they were ready to depart. Every passenger, excited.

But soldiers running toward the train suggested trouble. Nell observed the uniformed men boarding. The officer who the previous day had confiscated the luggage car for "the cause" came, too. Nell's heartbeat accelerated. What was the problem now? Again, the passengers were asked to come to the luggage coach. There, the officer was inspecting the luggage again. At his request, pieces were identified. Nell saw John at the back of the gathering. He avoided looking at her.

"This chest?" The officer questioned signaling John's.

"Mine." Coming forward he acknowledged it.

"I suppose a free slave?" the officer said, looking him up and down.

"Yes, sir. I am."

"Papers," the military man demanded with authoritarian tone.

John pulled a rugged, old envelope from an inside jacket pocket and from it an old, discolored paper which he gave to the military man saying: "My Stamped Certificate of Freedom."

The military looked at John again while examining the document.

"Open it," he ordered, signaling the trunk. John put the key in the locker, turning it and lifting the cover.

The officer checked the garments exposed. "Why carrying woman's clothing?"

"A female relative is sending these dresses to another family member."

"Anyway, how I know you are the person named on this paper and not a runaway slave?"

The opportunity came to Nell to be of great assistance to an acquaintance.

"I know him," she said advancing to them.

"Miss, we meet again." The officer faced her. "This man, his name?"

"John Smith," she answered. To erase any doubt, she added, "My father's business uses his services. That is why I know him."

The officer glanced around, obviously disappointed. He returned the paper to John. So, the denouncement of runaway slaves on the train was not accurate. Probably the fact John was the only black on board was the origin of the information.

"Officer," Nell said, sensing an opportunity to end the inquest, "why am I here? Was not my luggage already checked? Haven't the passengers of this train gone through enough mischief?"

More than one lady present assented, voicing their approval of Nell's words. The military man had no new argument. He dismissed the gathering and left with his escort.

At last, the engine was set, the train rolled from the small station. Nell watched the outside as they passed by hospital tents built on the outskirts of town. By the number of them, the amount of hospitalized soldiers must be high; it would keep the nurses busy. She remembered Vilma, her old friend. Now, better informed, her sentiments of culpability attributable to Gabriel and Vilma were diminished. The crime committed was far less punishable. Later she would certainly think on that matter again.

The nurses and volunteers were truly busy. The number of wounded soldiers increased so rapidly that construction of new facilities did not stop. The experience Vilma had acquired assisting her father in his medical practice was valuable training for treating wounded patients. Now she had the opportunity of becoming independent, cutting her ties with Roseville. After all, that was not a happy chapter in her life.

Wounded, sick soldiers arrived daily at the recently opened hospital. News of the medical institution spread quickly in the neighborhood, many taking advantage of the new opportunity for petty business.

Vilma was fitting the last contingent of young men admitted, rushing from one bed to the next, evaluating their health conditions.

"Hello, soldier," smiling she saluted the young man resting in bed.

"Sergeant," he corrected her.

"Already promoted?"

"Yes, after my first battle."

"Congratulations," Vilma said seating on the bed, checking his wrapped left leg.

"Unfortunately, I was shot too soon."

"With fighters so brave," she replied, "the war will end soon."

Finishing removing the bandage, she inspected the wound. "The bullet did fracture the bone, but not much." She cleaned and then covered the injured leg. "I'll keep an eye on you, Sergeant . . . ?"

"Greenfield, Dexter."

"Are you from around here?"

"Well, yes. Roseville is not far away."

"What a small world. I lived in that town lately."

She stood, wrote in a notebook and put it back inside her pocket.

Sergeant Dexter looked at her. He knew almost everybody around town; at least, he thought. "I have never seen you. Where did you live?" he asked.

"It was a short time. The house was on the outskirts of Roseville. I did not visit town frequently."

Dexter was intrigued. A young woman living in his home town and he never saw her?

Vilma, suspecting the questions going on the patient's head, did not wait any longer. "I'll be back later. Do not move your leg too much." She picked up the utility tray and stepped to the next bed.

The smooth motion of the train provided relaxation. The long waiting had caused anxiety to many. To be on the move again restored confidence and friendliness to all aboard. It was late afternoon when John Smith came to Nell's compartment.

"Miss Nell, thank you so much," he acknowledged his gratitude . . .

"John, I am glad to help you."

"It is not good to talk to me in public."

"I know; anyway, it does not worry me," she replied.

"We will be leaving at the next railway station," John informed her with low voice.

"Are they still inside the suitcase?" she questioned.

"Yes."

"Can they breathe?"

"Yes; if needed, they can open small holes."

"What a relief!"

"Miss Nell, will you please allow them to change clothes here early tomorrow?" John asked, lowering his voice a little more. "If they come off the train well dressed, less suspicious."

"Permission granted," she gladly agreed.

"From there we'll travel west; more facilities, you know and finally we'll go north."

"That's a long trip, John."

He nodded. "Miss, I must leave now. When all is ready, I'll come back."

Nell was already awaked when John knocked at the door. The young black couple and John rushed in. John gave them clothing to put on and he and Nell stepped outside while they changed. Moments later, the train stopped at a railway station. It was still dark and no one around. The young couple came out of the compartment looking completely different. Nobody could claim that they were last night John's shabby companions. Nell watched them leave the train with a wide smile, shining eyes, no need to say anything. The couples' faces said it all as they joined John stepping to the wooden plank. Nell went back into her compartment, sat at the window and stared out at the surroundings, listened the noises of the creatures of the wild joining the whistling sound of the steam released by the train's engine. A well-dressed black man with a stovepipe hat came, embraced John calling him 'Simon.' He also greeted the young couple and then John came back on the train. Nell opened the door and invited him to step in. He kissed Nell's hand. "I always will be at your orders, Miss."

Nell was moved by the chivalry gesture and the sincere gratitude. "We put your clothing back into your suitcase. No damage."

"That is all right, John. I hope to see you soon in Boston."

A whistle blow announced the departure of the train. John rapidly disembarked the cars already moving. Nell went to the window and watched as the small station shrunk in the distance. A group on the platform waved.

The Gilbert mansion's daily routine became more and more predictable. Gabriel spent long hours at his father's office, even after all matters were taken care of. He sat there with no desire to go out. Anne dedicated most of her day to Edna. Her health was delicate, and she would often skip dinner. Cecil and Gabriel were often alone. LaBelle was busier than ever, occasionally sending Clydette to assist Anne. Aunt Mabel came frequently, avoiding unpleasant topics of discussion, especially with Gabriel. She helped Anne taking care of her mother; sometimes she made them laugh with her witty sayings, bringing relaxation to the heavy atmosphere that had descended over the once vibrant, happy Southern family.

Cecil Gilbert's regular visitors gradually disappeared. The news from the battleground sent mixed signals. Many victories later became costly losses. Notices of wounded or dead soldiers soon circulated in cities and towns, recalling to the people's minds the reality of war. The optimistic sentiment previously displayed everywhere gradually changed to worried faces.

In short time the hospital's tent was crowded. The casualties admitted rapidly filled its capacity. Consequently, supplies often ran short, forcing the attending personnel to improvise and find replacements. Vilma prepared an outside blaze to boil water where she could wash and disinfect the hospital bedding and linens so they could be used again. She collected wood from nearby yards, sometimes helped by a black boy six or seven years old who hung around curiously.

"There is not much damage to the bone," Vilma explained, covering Dexter's wounded leg with new bandage. "Soon you will be fine."

Dexter looked at her. He still wondered how they had not met living in the same town. "Where did you live in Roseville?" he bluntly asked again.

"I already told you," she said holding back nervousness, eyes on her work. "Outside of town."

"I grew up there. I know everyplace," Dexter insisted.

Vilma cut the bandage and started to fasten it. She knew sooner or later it would come back . . . "I lived far opposite the train station. The house with white fence and Spanish moss trees."

Dexter opened his mouth and eyes grew wide. That was his good friend family's property. He controlled himself. "Do you know Gabriel Gilbert?" he asked as calmly as possible.

"Yes," she said picking up the supplies tray. Avoiding his eyes, Vilma left.

Nell concentrated on reading. The train must be in a hurry now since there were fewer stops and went through small hamlets at full speed. The outside view was often similar, quiet as if everybody had abandoned land, cabins and houses. The effects of the turmoil were evident everywhere.

There was no better way to dissipate the unpleasant panorama and forget the wondrous memory of that bounteous countryside admired not so long ago but keeping eyes inside. As the train moved northward the appearance and manners of the passengers changed accordingly. Nell had plenty of time to think and reflect.

Once the train had crossed the rebels' territory, the outside became a pleasure to see: valleys, trees, bushes, flowers, and vegetation at full splendor. Here the destruction of war had not reached. No delays, heavy military presence or schedule changes. Finally, the train arrived at the Boston terminal. Nell breathed relieved. To see familiar streets, houses and faces restored something missing inside; life, as she knew it, came back, filling her soul. Completing the circle of reviving past emotions she at last embraced her father, still convalescing and her mother, thrilled to see her back home after a few but long years. And Susan also.

Dexter questioned no more the presence of Vilma in Roseville. In his circle personal issues were a top private matter; only the people involved spoke about it. Out of respect, nobody else would mention an affair. He was aware of her being there but never discussed this with Gabriel.

A doctor and his assistants were reviewing patients. They stopped at Dexter's bed. The assistant removed the bandage exposing red flesh and blood. The doctor inspected the wound; looking around he saw Vilma a few beds away and called her.

"Yes, Dr. Garfield?

"This wound is not healing well. Disinfect, clean and cover it."

"Yes, doctor."

The professionals continued to the next bed. Vilma picked up a supply tray from a table and came back to Dexter. Soaking a cotton ball, she applied it to the wound causing Dexter to squirm; Vilma held his leg tight. She continued cleaning the wound, removing blood and covered it with a fresh bandage. She walked away with the medical tray.

"Thank you, Miss Nurse," Dexter said smiling. She turned her head, returning his gratitude.

The next day a new group of soldiers arrived forcing the already crowded ward to tighten again. Dexter was transferred to another facility, out of reach of Vilma. He was disappointed.

"Sergeant, you are stable; all is fine."

"Sorry. I'd just feel much better if you take care of me," he said.

"I'll come and see you. Satisfied?"

Dexter was not, but rules were rules. A military man should know this. "Promise, Miss Vilma?"

"Cross my heart."

Cecil Gilbert was preoccupied. The effects of war were felt by everyone. The prospects of a quick victory based on high-ranking officers from the United States Army resigning and accepting Confederate commissions were vanishing each day. Pessimism, although not acknowledged, was present.

"I do not know how long shipping cotton to Europe through Boston will continue," Cecil commented to Gabriel, his voice low, lacking the positive, authoritarian tone that used to be so common. "Our ports are not secure. The naval blockade is real. But I'm afraid to be accused of treason because we are using a Northern city." Cecil stopped. He looked at his quiet companion. "What do you think?"

"Keep doing it and stop when necessary," Gabriel responded.

"For goodness sake, Son. This is serious matter. How can you be so indifferent?" Cecil complained. He stood up and paced.

"I have never been good in business matters, Father."

"And this behavior is doing any good to you?"

"Right now, I do not care."

Anne came into the room, excited and nervous. She said her mother was very sick. The two men followed her to Edna's rooms. Cecil looked at the pale woman resting in bed. Gabriel touched her forehead. "Father, she needs a doctor."

Over the next days the Gilbert mansion was in constant, noiseless activity. Edna seemed to improve one day; the next she would fall back to ill health. Anne, Aunt Mabel, and LaBelle were constantly at her side, covering all her needs, providing company and the best possible care.

A buggy was always ready to pick up a doctor. Finding one that wanted to come to the country town was difficult after the insurrection began. The war had monopolized the medical professionals, their services categorized not only humanitarian but patriotic. Medicines and instructions given by the doctors Gabriel could find were strictly followed; no detail or suggestion was overlooked.

Nevertheless, Edna never recovered her health. Peacefully, with the family around her, she passed away.

Well-dressed slaves carried the bier through the grand entrance of the mansion. Behind followed Cecil, Anne, Gabriel and Aunt Mabel, holding hands then came Darlene and relatives, Dexter's parents and Cecil's associates and acquaintances. LaBelle was crying, and Clydette, standing at the main door, watched the funeral procession silently. Reaching the road to town, the family mourners and accompanying groups in carriages followed the marching men carrying the corpse through Roseville down the main street. Men took off their hats and women made the sign of the cross, watching in silence. At the cemetery, they endured the painful moment of lowering the coffin and throwing flowers and earth. Cecil was quiet; he stood grave and close to the monument. Anne, Gabriel and Aunt Mabel next to him.

Anne noticed a man walking behind the tombstones, looking at them. He called her signaling with his hand. She stepped apart, and the man rapidly approached her.

"Miss, my condolences," he said ceremoniously, taking off his hat.

"You know me?" Anne asked.

"Not until now," the man responded.

"Who are you?"

"Ralph Wallace, Anson's father."

Anne was shocked; this was so unexpected.

"My son asked for you," the man said.

She could not speak, her emotions running high.

"Anson sent a letter; he says has written frequently to you."

Aunt Mabel, noticing Anne was talking to a stranger, walked over to them. Anson's father, seeing her coming, bowed his head slightly and went away, disappearing between the monuments.

On their way back home in the carriage driven by Wade, nobody spoke.

Normalcy returned slowly to the mansion. Days later Anne came to her father's office.

"Any letter for me," she inquired.

Cecil, face pale, raised his eyes. Recovering his stamina, he directed his attention to the papers scattered over the executive desk. "All mail received have been delivered," he said in a tone lower than he was accustomed to using, even in these depressed days. Anne left knowing it was useless to argue. Anyway, her expectations were clearly shown.

Francis Dumont was gaining strength, feeling better 'thanks to the presence of my daughter.' Resting in the ample terrace, he was wrapped up to the waist with blankets, Nell at his side on a patio chair enjoying the breeze.

"Good afternoon," James Fitzgerald saluted coming in. "Looking great, Francis. Soon you will be back working," he added shaking the partner's hand and smiling at Nell.

"He is not going to the office till I approve it," Nell answered, pretending seriousness.

"I wish when ill, someone at my bedside spoiled me that much, Francis," Mr. Fitzpatrick said. "I guess I must accept reality. I will be alone, with no boss, for a long, long time." He grinned.

Mary Dumont came; it was time for Francis to take his medication. James Fitzgerald said good-bye. Mary pushed her husband's wheelchair inside the house. The temperature was falling, and the convalescent man did not need to add new conditions to his health. Susan arrived, joining Nell in the terrace.

"Did you see Vilma in Roseville?"

Nell had commented the affair to Susan but not to her parents; since Vilma was a friend there was no need to darken her memory. "No, in the South they follow special rules and customs," Nell replied. "They have mutual agreements. Some private situations are never mentioned, avoiding bitter explanations. My parents-in-law are separated. Even at the beginning I noticed their behavior rare, it took me months to confirm it. Gabriel and I did not talk about it. This matter was never openly discussed."

Susan grimaced. "Anyway, it is disgusting because you know of it."

"True, but Southerners handle delicate situations very cleverly."

A white female servant came and gave Nell a letter.

"It is from Gabriel."

"Nell, he already misses you."

As Nell silently read the letter, her face changed. Susan noticed it but kept quiet. Nell stopped reading and dropped her arms, setting down the letter. She looked away, taking a deep breath. "Gabriel's mother died," she said slowly, sorrows in her voice.

"Oh my God!" Susan exclaimed.

"I should have been there," Nell lamented, envisioning the mansion at such a tragic time.

"We must tell the bees," Susan said reminding an old New England tradition.

Vilma went to an adjacent tent searching for medical supplies. The number of patients depleted the stocks rapidly. She knew replacements had arrived. Not finding any there, she moved to the next facility, the doctor's quarters. Luckily, nobody was there. On the far side of the room she saw new boxes. She went to them; bending to the ground to open one, she heard people coming. She kept out of sight.

"We are losing too many patients."

Vilma recognized Dr. Garfield's voice. He continued. "Infections and shattered bones are not healing properly. We do not have enough antiseptics." The assistants present muttered agreement. "We must stop this," Dr. Garfield continued. "Gangrene is killing more soldiers than bullets. We have no alternative but to amputate infected limbs with no signs of healing. The supply of ether and chloroform received will provide the needed anesthesia. I'll be there and will answer any questions."

Everyone present approved of the plan. They left. Vilma found and picked up the medical material she sought and went back to her ward, distributing the supplies between different stations.

The next day, a long line of patients were at the surgery facility tent, suggesting great activity there. Vilma finished with an injured man and then went toward the exit. She looked at the soldiers chatting while they waited. One man waved to her. She nodded her head to return the salutation; it was Dexter. She approached him.

"Are you going to surgery?" she asked.

"That is right. They asked to come."

"Follow me."

Abruptly she pulled him by the arm, making him to walk as fast as he could. They entered the next tent and Vilma checked around. At the end of the tent was one empty bed. She told him to lie down there and to wait for her. She came back momentarily with a medical supplies tray and sat at his side, taking the dirty bandage off Dexter's leg.

"Dexter, your wound is not that bad. I will disinfect it three or even four times a day if necessary to control the infection," she explained, talking as fast as her hands worked. "My father was good healing wounds. Sometimes doctors go to extreme procedures; we can succeed applying regular treatments. Trust me; do not go to any place without checking with me."

Dexter listened with attention. Her eagerness and dedication won his admiration; even the pain from the cleaning and scrubbing was less painful.

"This is not my assigned area," she continued, wrapping the wound. "I will talk with the person in charge and explain your case. When there is space in my ward, I'll transfer you."

Carrying the medical tray, Vilma left; no time for Dexter to say anything. He saw her a few beds away talking to a nurse, probably the one in charge.

Early next morning Vilma woke up Dexter with good news; she had managed to add one bed to her section. She transferred him quickly without causing suspicion.

"Dexter, when Dr. Garfield and his assistants come," she advised, "avoid them. Go down the aisle, outside if necessary."

"I appreciate very much your interest in my health," Dexter responded. "I will do whatever you say, but why did you take me out of the surgery ward? I heard wounds heal faster after Dr. Garfield's operations."

Vilma moved down, stopping at the end of the bed. She pulled the sheet tight. "Dr. Garfield is frustrated with casualties in the hospital. He has no other recourse to improve the results but applying radical methods."

Dexter accepted her reasoning. He already felt more secure being her around. So far she had shown capability and dedication to her profession.

As promised, Vilma frequently treated Dexter's wounded leg. Also, she started a plan following her father's experience and practice adding fruit juices to Dexter's diet. She managed to get oranges, limes, grapefruits and lemons through the young black boy who was sneaking around the camp.

A couple days later, Dr. Garfield and associates walked into Dexter's ward checking the patients. Dexter got up as soon as he saw them; with the help of a wooden cane Vilma had given him, he crossed behind beds, walking as fast as his legs allowed, entering the next facility. There he saluted some old companions; farther on, he saw a man he had met while on line for surgery. He wanted to say hello but the sadness on the man's face stopped him. Then noticed he had one leg missing. Dexter kept moving, eyes scanning from side to side. Here, a man with one arm amputated; there, a leg. Suddenly it dawned on him why Vilma had taken such special measures in his treatment.

Carrying a basketful of dirty linen sheets, Vilma walked out of the hospital to the boiling water spot. She emptied the basket into the pot and then added wood to the fire.

"Mizz . . . Mizz." An old black woman, pulling a black boy by his arm, approached Vilma. "'Dis boy stealeh fum yo'sef?" she asked seriously.

Vilma, surprised, looked at them; she recognized the boy as the one who has been going around, helping her and providing citrus fruits.

"What?" she asked first confused because did not understand the woman but soon realized the situation. "No, he did not steal from me. I paid him for fruits; he is a good boy!"

The face of the woman changed. Loosening the boy, she looked at Vilma. "Den . . . wuz bizness, eh?"

"Yes, he always helps me."

"'Un my fambly no thief, hum'!" She left as fast as she had appeared, still holding the boy.

The physician in charge of Francis Dumont paid his patient a visit. Mary Dumont and Nell listened to his explanations concerning care and medications. The reason for the continued illness remained elusive; the doctor did everything he could. He pointed out that the daily reduction of fever was a formidable sign for hope.

The slow but continued increase in strength Francis showed during the passing weeks helped restore tranquility and peace of mind to the disrupted Dumonts, allowing Nell to relax. She focused on reviewing other personal matters on hold but equally disturbing, waiting to be resolved. The presence of Susan was another relief since Nell had absolute confidence in her. She could open up and expose her feelings, the problems hurting her life. Also, Gabriel proved to be a constant, faithful writer, even if simply informing his wife of casual activities and the daily routine around the mansion. He never mentioned their separation or asked when she would return.

Nell did not answer him promptly. She wrote mainly referring to her father's health condition; she had no other messages. And since the news from the war, today not at all favorable to the South, it was better not to mention it.

It was late at night when Vilma came to Dexter's bed carrying a medical tray. She sat at his side. "Dexter, wake up."

"What?"

"I need to remove the infected flesh. First, drink the lemonade," she said softly.

He took the jug from her hands and drank the juice while she prepared medical material on the tray.

"You must be quiet," she advised in a low voice. "I am going to cut tissue; you must not complain if it's painful. I'm sorry; I could not get enough anesthesia."

He sat up, asking, "*Why must we do this now?*"

"I should not do this without superior authorization."

Vilma removed the bloody bandage from his leg and applied a cold liquid to the wound while Dexter watched. The tent was almost without candle light, most of the patients were sleeping. Vilma, with a scissors cut the infected flesh. Dexter jumped a little; she held him, cleaned the blood coming from the injured leg and then wrapped it quickly. Silently, she left, carrying the supplies tray.

When Vilma came later, Dexter was not happy. She changed the bandage.

"It hurts a lot," he complained.

"That's because it is healing," she explained.

"But it feels like a burning flame!"

"That will pass. The tibia was slightly split; it will recover faster if you keep quiet."

"How long will I have to stay in bed? I have been here long time."

"And it would be longer if you had surgery," she responded, moving to the next bed with the tray in her hands.

Joining customary activities helped Gabriel to go back to semi-regular life. Cecil wanted Wade close to him, to get updated news. Many contradictory war reports were going around. To hear the version closer to reality was extremely important. News that Northern armies were fighting their way down the Mississippi River was alarming.

Gabriel's presence at the plantation was imperative. The liberation of slaves in territories the Union's took control over made many brave souls lose sleep. Consequently, militias, vigilantes, and armed patrol volunteer groups formed everywhere. The Southerner's patriotic sentiment and belief in their fortitude somehow started to crack. A void was evident. The Confederacy so far had not gained global diplomatic recognition; the high qualifications of their officers in command had not sent a clear, decisive message to the Southern cause which would have opened the road to victory.

"One last thing, Gabriel." Cecil called on his son's way out after the early morning meeting, "As planned, the next shipment will go through Boston. I am asking our clients in England to remit payment to Mr. Dumont. I have already advised him. Nell's father will keep these funds till I request them. He is a person we can trust. When you write to your wife, please mention this."

"Her father is sick. Still you want to embark through them? We almost lost the cargo last time."

"I know, but it is yet legal. Let us try again, even though I doubt we could do it next time."

Wade walked in with rapid, long strides. Excited, he gave them the news of a nearby battle fought. There were big causalities and rumors circulated in town that among the dead were soldiers from Roseville. The telegraph office will post the information when received. People were already gathering there. Gabriel left; notices like this spread fast, increasing nervousness among the free and slaves.

Late that afternoon, Cecil received the unannounced visit of Aunt Mabel. She sat facing him; her constant, friendly smile not there.

"I just read at the telegraph station," she started, her voice breaking, "the notice of the battle fought you surely heard where local men died." She stopped, taking in air and breathing deeply.

"Relax, Aunt Mabel," Cecil said. "We are at war. Do you want water?"

"Two of the dead soldiers are from Roseville," she continued paying no attention to him. "They will be mourned tomorrow in town, following a military burial." She looked straight at the quiet, secure man. "One of the soldiers killed is . . . Anson Williams."

Not long ago that name had meant anything to Cecil. Today, it was a hard blow to his senses. He tilted his head back, eyes wide open, a series of conflicting emotions crossing his mind.

Grasping his hands hard, eyes on the pale woman facing him, he couldn't produce a word. This must be true. Aunt Mabel would not say something like that unless she was completely sure. Cecil stood and walked around, releasing the hot heat coming out his body. "Anne must not know this," he finally said, overcoming the stupor of the news, coming back to the executive chair.

The good Aunt looked at him in disbelief. Was he insane? How could this be kept secret?

"Not a word, Aunt Mabel. Do you hear me?" Cecil ordered the shattered woman.

He must be out of his mind! she thought. Distressed, Aunt Mabel started crying. She took a handkerchief from her purse. "Cecil, I cannot do it. Anson's father was there. He wanted to come. I begged him not to; he accepted when I promised to tell Anne." Shaking, tears running down her face, Aunt Mabel looked at the now worried man. Taking a fresh breath, she asked, "Did Anne get letters from him?"

"Of course not! I personally took care of that," the master admitted. "She is my daughter. I will never consent for people of low-class background around her."

"My goodness, Cecil! This is no time for superfluous social rules. The boy is dead!"

Cecil squirmed in the seat, his eyes full of anguish, wanting his will to prevail. But today worthless compared with the shocking fact. Aunt Mabel, aware of the turmoil inside him, stayed there, waiting for the storm to lose strength. She saw dampness in Cecil's eyes but would not dare to say that.

Moments later, she went out of the office without saying where she was going. Cecil probably knew. Slowly, with heavy steps she went upstairs wishing never to reach the top level. No needed to call Anne; she had heard her steps. Smiling, she opened the door, embraced her Aunt asking why the sad face as they went inside the apartment.

LaBelle carrying a pot came into the room. Anne was crying bitterly, lying on the bed with Aunt Mabel holding her hand. LaBelle served a hot beverage in a goblet and came to the bed. Aunt Mabel took the drinking glass and offered it to Anne. "Dear, drink this tea; it will calm your nerves. You know how good LaBelle's infusions are."

She drank slowly, gulp by gulp, holding her breath. The loyal servant stood apart, speechless.

As she had promised, Aunt Mabel came back the next day, going directly to Anne's rooms.

"I sent Clydette to town," Anne informed her. "She will find out when the corpses arrive. I am going to Anson's funeral."

The clear, resolute statement was the most disturbing one Aunt Mabel had ever heard from her niece.

Gabriel came. Holding Anne's face, he kissed her forehead. He left as silently as he had entered.

Early, at mid-morning, Clydette returned from Roseville with the wake information. The soldiers' coffins were lying in the meeting house and people were already gathering there. Anne put on the black dress she'd worn at Edna's burial and fixed a bonnet on her head. She went toward the stairs followed by a scared Aunt Mabel. Firmly, head high, Anne came down. When reaching the ground level, she saw LaBelle and Clydette coming out Cecil's private office.

"Miss Anne, sorry. Master Gilbert ordered no carriage for you. He said you are not allowed to go to Roseville," LaBelle informed her holding back tears. Cecil came out of his office.

"LaBelle," Anne retorted, "I need no authorization from anyone to go where I want." The clear tone of her fearless voice froze Aunt Mabel's blood. "Have the coach ready."

"You are going nowhere!" The loud voice of the master shook the hall.

"I am going to Roseville," Anne riposted.

"You disobey me?" Cecil screamed, hands clutching each other tightly.

LaBelle, pulling Clydette by an arm, rushed to the end of the hall and outside.

"I am not a little girl. It is my desire and I am going to Roseville," Anne boldly replied

"You, too?" Cecil said, biting back his impulses. "Your brother already asked me to be patient with you. He also disapproves of my judgment. This is the effect of Nell's influence!"

"She has nothing to do with this," Anne affirmed.

"Of course she is responsible," Cecil rapidly rebuked. "Never my children had questioned my orders till she came!"

"It is because your resolutions do not agree with our opinions."

"Do not agree? What is next, ignoring my authority?" he asked, pacing.

"I will," Anne responded, "if it is used against my welfare." She took a step forward.

"You will not go out of this house!" Cecil walked ahead, barring her way. Aunt Mabel almost fainted; she raised her hands to hold, protect Anne but she was out of her reach.

"I am going to Anson's funeral. Nobody is going to stop me."

Anne's voice left no doubt. A cold tremor shook Cecil's body: he had heard his own commanding tone in his daughter's voice. "No, I will not allow you to mix with members of undistinguished families," he declared.

"They have not destroyed my happiness as you have done!" Anne's bitter, sad words filled the room.

"There is no carriage!"

"I can walk."

"You will not . . . over my dead body!" Eyes red, perspiring, shaking and fists clenched, Cecil seemed he was going to explode.

His daughter firmly faced him. "To be with Anson's body today will be the last happy moment for the rest of my life. Nobody is going to stop me. I will never speak to you again. Get out of my way!"

Hitting shoulder against shoulder, Anne brushing him off walked to the front door. Cecil, shuddering, trying to react could not move. Aunt Mabel, recovering from the frightening scene ran following Anne, even though at this moment she was a stranger to her.

The meeting house was crowded. Everybody turned their heads to look at the two ladies holding hands as they came in. Nobody had expected any Gilberts at that gathering. The room was festooned with black crepe. At the center, two coffins wrapped with Confederacy flags rested on catafalques, guarded by soldiers. When Anne got closer, Mr. Wallace, Anson's father, advanced to her. They embraced and cried tears of sorrow. Anne, shaking, touched the coffin, rested her forehead on it for a few moments. Then she sat facing the coffins, Aunt Mabel on one, Mr. Wallace on the other side. People came along paying their respects to the deceased and their relatives.

The procession, long and dusty, was led by a detachment of troops followed by the funeral wagon. A great number of citizens of Roseville joined the grieving families on the road to the resting place. At the cemetery entrance, Anne got two long-stemmed white roses from a vendor standing by. Walking, holding hands with Anson's father, they followed the uneven path to the grave. They watched the coffins as they were lowered and covered with earth while shots were fired, causing the gathered people to flinch. Anne, crying, laid a flower on top of the tomb. When the ceremony was over, she went to her family's mausoleum. She placed the second flower on the white slab.

"This is for your mother," Aunt Mabel guessed.

"No, it is for my father. He died today," Anne answered. Her aunt shook.

On their way out, Mr. Wallace thanked Aunt Mabel for advising Anne.

"I would like to keep in touch," Anne begged him.

"That is not possible," he replied. "I'm going back to Kentucky; no war there."

"I'm sorry to hear that. We could have been friends."

"We already are," he responded. "Anson's officer told me he'd never had a more dedicated, braver soldier who obeyed orders with such exemplary discipline. If he'd lived longer, he would have advanced very high in the military."

"I have no doubt," Anne agreed.

"He said he wrote frequently to you."

This brought fresh tears to Anne's eyes. "Ralph, his last letters never reached me."

They stopped at the cemetery entrance. As people filed out, they saluted again the parents of the other dead soldier, a rustic, humble couple who bashfully said good-bye.

"Anne, your carriage?" Mr. Wallace asked.

"Yes," Aunt Mabel answered, checking around, "it must be near; thank God I had it. Where are Clydette and my buggy?"

"I'm glad. I have no carriage," Mr. Wallace apologized.

"That's fine, Ralph. My servant must be coming soon," Anne replied, looking around.

"There she is!" Aunt Mabel announced, waving one arm to call her attention. Clydette, driving the buggy stopped close to them.

"Miss Anne," Mr. Wallace said, holding her hands, "I will always remember you. I hope we will meet again."

"I am very grateful," Anne responded. "I will pray for Anson and you."

They embraced, tears coming to their eyes, living testimony of sad moments shared which forever would be deep inside in their hearts.

Mr. Wallace thanked Aunt Mabel again; he helped them to get inside the buggy which Clydette drove down the trail toward town. The two women waved the solitary man standing still, returning their farewell.

The Gilbert mansion, already quiet, became gloomier. Gabriel spent long hours in the fields, since Wade was absent due to time-consuming work ordered by Cecil, sometimes putting in more hours than necessary.

Gabriel came home tired which helped him suppress thoughts of his personal problems and retired early, leaving Cecil alone since Anne, as decided, no longer spoke to him and firmly rejected her brother's requests to join them for dinner.

Nell and Susan met almost every afternoon, sitting in the back terrace, letting their thoughts run free, exchanging ideas and desires.

"I was happy, but do not ask what made me feel that; I could not tell you," Nell said.

"Sorry I never wrote," Susan said regretfully. "I was always thinking that tomorrow I would do it, but I never did. Just like years ago in school. Whenever a teacher asked for something in writing, I never did it." She chuckled, and then grew serious. "Besides, the rebellion in the South closed any desire of travel."

"The countryside is beautiful, flowers, thick forests but war changed everything."

"Certainly it has. Even here the main topic is fighting. At meetings and gatherings, all that men talk about is weapons, battles and military operations."

"They should go down and see the destruction, the wounded soldiers," Nell suggested.

"Oh, yes, Nell. We have seen the casualties list and photographs of injured young men, giving me creepy flesh."

Nell shook her head mournfully. "That's the real face of war, Susan, the casualties."

"Many young men want to carry a gun and go to war."

"These are difficult times for everybody, Susan. Let us talk about more pleasant things. Tell me; is there anybody around that interest you?"

"All the men I know are engaged, married, or too old. And the young ones, the army is on their minds," Susan responded laughing.

"Some day things will change. I do not know when, but this cannot last forever."

"I hope it will end soon; time is running out, Nell."

Mary Dumont came walking fast. "Nell, your father is not well," she said almost crying.

A worried look came across Nell's face. "He was fine when I saw him not long ago."

"He has a fever again," Mary informed her.

"Send a servant to bring his doctor," Nell instructed standing up and walking into the house followed by her mother and Susan.

The plantations owners' primary attention was still focused on news from the battlefields. Hope of a short, victorious war effort had disappeared completely as the war dragged on. Local defense sources became the main concern, along with inflation and shortness of food supplies and all commodities.

"Dexter is still in a hospital," Cecil told Gabriel while lighting a cigar in the small parlor after having dinner. "His father came over this afternoon. They are worried."

"How is he doing?"

"He wrote he is improving. His wound is healing thanks to the nurse taking care of him but still needs medical care."

Gabriel was there to accompany his father. He had no desire to either talk or hear about the war but this was the only social moment they shared.

"Promise you will not enlist in the military," Cecil requested, his voice grave.

Gabriel looked at him. Firm, serene and proud, his hard aspect had somehow diminished. Instead, there was a measure of sadness on his father's face.

"I have no intention of leaving you," he responded.

The next morning, Gabriel left the mansion on horseback taking the trail to the plantation. Ahead was a long working day which he accepted since it kept his mind occupied, no time to think about his trouble with Nell. Wade, riding in the opposite direction, approached him, stopping close when they met.

"I took out four slave men from the plantation," he explained.

"That's fine." Gabriel urged his horse to continue.

"I sent them to Roseville," Wade added.

Gabriel stopped and turned to face the employee again, sensing he had more to report.

"Young Gabriel, Mr. Gilbert ordered that," Wade said with his earnest smile.

"Father wanted men in town?" Gabriel thought that was unusual.

"Well, it is not of my business." Wade paused, but he needed to say it. "Miss Flora Hobson is leaving Roseville. She needed help to move out."

Gabriel stared at the man perceiving his maliciousness. Suddenly he remembered Nell's words; she was right feeling uneasy about him. Pulling the reins, he directed his horse back toward the plantation. Wade's words kept coming to Gabriel's head. So, his father's mistress was going away now that Cecil was free. What could have happened? She was a demanding woman; Gabriel knew that. From the very beginning she had let everyone in Roseville to know who she was. She had gone away once before, but then she came back, apparently against Cecil's desires. So why was she departing now? Had Cecil asked her, or did she want something that Cecil had refused?

At dinner that night, Gabriel did not notice any change in Cecil's mood. He was quiet, but that was his typical attitude ever since Edna's death and Anne's retreat. Anyway, the existence of Miss Hobson had never been discussed between them, so it wasn't surprising that Cecil did not mention it now.

Francis Dumont's fever slowly receded once more and his weak condition seemed to improve, though his family kept a constant vigil. Inability to foresee more than one day ahead tested everyone nerves.

"Mother, if Father's sickness continues, we should find him another doctor," Nell advised.

"He is doing what he can, Nell. He was well recommended."

"This has been going on for months. Father should be better; instead, there is no steady recovery."

"I guess everybody is doing their best, daughter. Oh, how I miss Dr. Mullen."

"If I see no real signs of healing by next weeks, I will take Father to New York or somewhere else to have him treated."

Mary shook her head in disagreement. "This is not a good time for traveling, Nell."

"By train there is no danger; besides, in New York there is no fighting."

"Who's fighting?" Susan asked smiling as she walked onto the terrace.

"We are," Nell answered, embracing her friend and inviting her to sit.

"Hi, Mary. How is the patient?"

"Improving, Susan, I think."

"I see no recovery," Nell explained. "I was suggesting taking him to another city."

Mary interrupted, "Our medical professionals are highly esteemed, Nell."

"I don't question their competency, but Father is no better today than last week."

"Such a long trip will not hurt him?" Mary questioned.

"No, Mother. Trains are comfortable."

"If any of us can say that, it's Nell," Susan pointed out.

"Yes. The things a person learns during a trip," the young woman agreed.

"Romance, Nell? So far you haven't said much about the ride up here," Susan said with mysterious tone.

"Not that, Susan. I'm a married woman and they are at war."

Nell's mother brought the topic back around. "Anyway, today traveling is risky."

"I agree with you, Mary," Susan backed her.

"Let me see how Francis is doing," Mary said, standing up. "Refreshments, Susan?"

"No thanks, I'm all set."

Mary walked toward the entrance of the house, leaving the young pair alone, enjoying the fresh breeze that was coming from the countryside.

"I never imagined I was going to miss Roseville," Nell said, letting her heart speak. "If LaBelle were here, she could help Father with her medical infusions."

Susan gazed at her friend but kept silent, not disturbing her reminiscences.

From nearby towns and cities, a group of ladies were distributing presents to the injured soldiers. Vilma and other nurses helped the visiting women go to bed after bed, chatting with the wounded. Many ladies could not hide their shock when facing young men with amputated limbs. The medical team and nurses and soldiers thanked them at the end of the tour.

"What did you get?" Vilma asked Dexter.

"Sweets, magazines and newspapers."

"They donated linen sheets and pillows too. Let me bring you orange juice."

"Wait. As you suggested, I don't hide from the doctors or assistants any more. Dr. Garfield checked my leg today and said I will be discharged soon,"

"Great. Does that not make you happy?"

"Yes, I already sent a letter to my parents."

Vilma changed the topic. "We've run out of crutches. If supplies arrive soon, I will give you a set."

"My leaving doesn't worry me, but you," Dexter told her.

"Sergeant, I am fine. I enjoy my job and happy to see someone going home."

"Come with me."

Vilma looked intensely at him. She tried to understand the meaning of his words. What was on his mind, had developed inside him due to her behavior toward him? He surely knew why she lived in Roseville. A sad, painful thought crossed her mind, crushed the strong person she had became lately. Anyway, what right he had, how he could dare to make such a proposition? Rapidly she turned her back and walked away.

"Come back; let me explain!" Dexter called but she was too upset, deeply hurt to hear him.

When Vilma came for the next wound cleaning and changing of bandages, she started working without talking or looking at Dexter's face. She merely did the job professionally. Dexter needed to repair the unwanted damage done. "I apologize. I had no intention of hurting you. Believe me; I was sincere, honest, well-meaning thought."

Vilma stopped wrapping. Dexter had always seemed to be a straight, right man. Emotions inside less predominant. She finally accepting his apologies smiled looking at him. Finishing her job, rapidly she moved to the next patient.

The Gilbert mansion was no longer the place to meet, exchange information and be up-to-date in business and social activities in the community. Cecil, previously always busy, today spent hours alone, waiting for someone to step in to chat, just talk. The heavy toll of war pressing at every level had rapidly changed the Gilberts' style of living. Life, as they knew it, would never be the same.

"What happened to your face?" Gabriel asked his father at dinner, noticing a bruised area.

"Nothing. I fell."

"How was that?" Cecil's explanation did not satisfy him.

"Just on the floor," the old man answered bringing food to his mouth.

"Stumbled, hit something?"

"No, I was suddenly on the floor."

"Really? It happened that way?"

"Of course, a silly fall."

During the next morning meeting, Gabriel paid special attention to Cecil's movements. The previous day accident troubled him. Edna's death had made him a cautious man.

"Father, are you feeling well?" Gabriel noticed he seemed tired.

"I'm fine," Cecil responded. "Son, keep an eye on the cotton gin equipment," he said promptly to change the subject to business matters.

"I will, Father," Gabriel assured ready to leave.

"Wade will join you later," Cecil said standing up to come over but he lost balance; rapidly he placed his hands on the desk to avoid falling. Gabriel saw the struggling and rushed over, grabbing him by the arms, helped him to sit down.

"What happened?"

Cecil, short of breath, could not answer. He was sweating and pale. Gabriel pulled the ring bell for service and came back to Cecil who was recuperating.

"Feeling better?"

"Yes," Cecil said. Gabriel filled a glass with water from a pitcher on the desk. He gave it to Cecil, who drank a sip.

"Will you say it was nothing?" Gabriel said seriously, attentively looking at his father for clues as to the cause of such happening to a strong, healthy man.

"I do not know," the Master admitted. "I just blacked out."

"You need to see a doctor," Gabriel affirmed.

Cecil was confused, unable to respond. LaBelle came into the room.

"Get his bed ready," Gabriel instructed her. "He is going to rest."

The slave servant left as fast as she came to carry out the order. Gabriel helped Cecil to go upstairs and put him into bed. When the man did so without arguing, Gabriel knew the case was serious.

After leaving his father resting, Gabriel went to Anne's apartment. She was sitting on a chair facing the window, contemplating the surrounding forest. Gabriel looked at her, quiet; she did not seem to be aware of his presence. He stood next to her, watching the outside as well. "Anne, I want to talk to you."

She did not answer or even move a muscle. Gabriel put his hands inside the trousers' pockets. "Father is sick. He needs to see a doctor," he said slowly, searching for the right words. "This time

I'll take him to a nearby city as soon as possible; will not wait as when mother got sick."

Anne did not move. Her eyes were fixed on the trees moving with the wind.

"The trip could be short or long," Gabriel continued. "It depends on finding a doctor. Anyway, someone must travel with us to help him."

He paused knowing he was reaching a crucial point. Turning his eyes, he checked Anne's visage to see how the message was received. There was no clear sign. "LaBelle would be the perfect companion but then this house would be disrupted since no one else can handle her job. Then, she is eliminated. That leads us to Clydette who is not trained well enough for this task." Gabriel stopped to regain his breath and strength for the heavy burden coming. "I have no choice but to ask you to come with us."

Anne turned slowly her head to Gabriel. What he saw was a somber, aged face with a dull expression. A sad, chill sentiment came over his chest. He had never seen his sister like this, so lifeless.

"I have no father." The voice matched her appearance.

"Not true, Anne."

"My father," she continued, ignoring him: "I buried months ago."

Gabriel, pacing impatiently, trying hard not to lose his temper, came back, kneeling at her side, grasping Anne's chair arms. With his most friendly tone, he repeated his request: "Anne, sister, Father needs you. Please!"

She looked firmly at him, something resembling a smile surfacing on her unexpressive face. "I'll do anything for you, but for somebody who is dead, there is nothing I can do," she said immediately turning her eyes back to the outside wilderness.

Gabriel arranged to travel along with Cecil who, unexpectedly, did not refuse. He instructed LaBelle to watch the house and to take care of Anne and left Wade in charge of the plantation, specifically advising him that if a slave needed to be punished, he should use discretion. They left on a sunny day, taking the daily train crossing town going north, searching for medical assistance.

The trip did not bring pleasant moments. The only sight towns and cities offered to visitors were the burden of war. Military men everywhere. The merry, cheerful Southern charm had vanished. Fortunately, in Augusta medical practitioners were available. Cecil was pleased since he did not want to go too far north. Soon Gabriel made the necessary contacts and various doctors examined Cecil. The diagnosis was that he had a mild heart condition, prescribing rest and medications.

Gabriel and Cecil returned home right away. Once back in Roseville, Gabriel instructed LaBelle to take care of Cecil and to delegate all other matters. Prepared or not, Clydette had to carry the heavy burden of taking care of the mansion along with the assistants currently helping and under LaBelle's supervision.

In Cecil's office, a tray with medications was added on the executive desk to the one with glassware and water. "These tablets, two every morning," Gabriel said to LaBelle, showing her the bottle. Clydette, at a distance, also heard the instructions.

Gabriel picked up another prescription. "This potion, at midday." He put it back, picked up a new container. "These, one before dinner. The doctor said he must take everything regularly, no missing allowed, do you understand?"

"Yes, Young Gabriel," the attentive LaBelle answered.

"This is very important," Gabriel said, showing her another bottle and pointing to the name on the label. "Nitroglycerin. One tablet under the tongue at bedtime."

"I see it," LaBelle confirmed.

"In case of an emergency, he can take another," Gabriel instructed.

"I know, I know." Nodding, the servant assented.

"Father will be coming here," Gabriel continued. "Do not bring to him any problem of the mansion; I will manage them. Also, if he is not feeling well he shall receive no visitors."

"Yes, Young Gabriel," she agreed.

"If you have any questions, ask me," Gabriel finished. Confident the old, faithful servant had understood everything.

There were many people out in Charleston's streets, taking advantage of a fresh breeze blowing from the countryside. Also, a relative stillness of news from the war crowded the roads with carriages, couples and children crossing from one side of the street to the other. Tension was low at the moment but the nervousness shown by the rapid walking of pedestrians was a reminder of the perils of the times. The city, since a Confederate transportation and communication center, became a busy hub.

Vilma and Dexter, pacing slowly enjoyed a relaxing afternoon. She, admiring this new world; he, walking on crutches at her side.

"Everything is so interesting. I could go on for hours and hours."

"I'm hungry," Dexter said, stopping momentarily. "We need to find a restaurant."

"You know of any around?"

"I believe there is one down there," he said signaling ahead.

The crowded sidewalk did not allow Dexter, evidently not completely recovered, to go faster. Vilma, slowing her steps, kept close to him. Suddenly, she stopped. The man coming ahead was too familiar.

"What is it?" Dexter questioned.

The man, getting closer, saw Vilma too. He hurriedly changed direction, turning and stepping into the street.

"Stop! Stop him!" Vilma shouted rushing to the street, pointing at the now running man. The heavy traffic halted him in the middle of the road. With no place to go, Vilma reached him.

"Please, Miss Mullen!" the man implored her.

"I am glad you remember me!" Vilma grabbed him by his jacket's arm, returning both to the sidewalk.

"Forgive me!" the man said, almost crying.

"This man," Vilma informed Dexter, "stole my inheritance."

"Miss, I am so sorry," the robber apologized shaking. "I paid hard for that mistake, Miss Mullen!"

Vilma did not listen to his repentance. "I want you in jail! Where is a police officer?"

"Miss, please! If I could, I would return everything," the thief said, bitterly crying.

A few curious men watched at a distance. There was no authority personality in sight. Vilma got impatient. "Dexter, you are a military man. Arrest him."

Dexter looked at her. She was right and had reasons to be mad. "Do not move," Dexter ordered the crying man. There was little he could do; he needed both hands to handle the crutches and due to wearing a warfare uniform, he could at least scare the culprit till he could found help.

"I have already been punished. The war ruined me," the man explained in a piteous tone. "I lost everything. I am poor again."

Vilma looked at him; he had no fancy clothes, any aspect of wealth. On the contrary, fatigue, anguish and sorrow present in his eyes.

"Believe me, Miss, I regretted a thousand times what I did. I have not lived one day without feeling miserable, wanting to pay you back." The man fidgeted nervously as he revealed his ordeal. Really, he did not appear to have a prosperous life. Vilma looked at him again, thinking that maybe he was telling the plain truth. Nothing seemed contradictory but confirming.

"You lost everything?" she repeated questioningly.

"Exactly, Miss Mullen," he confirmed breathing heavily. "I may end up in prison; I owe too much." His voice sounded sincere, scared. "Please, let me go."

Dexter checked around. No authorities were present, near or far. They did not know the location of a courthouse or where to go and file an accusation. The people standing at a distance observing the quarrel were dispersing slowly.

"What should I do?" Vilma asked Dexter.

"It's your decision," Dexter answered. "Whatever you say, I will agree with."

The chances of finding this man again were slim and the damages he'd done were too painful for Vilma to ignore. Unfortunately the place and time were not propitious.

"How did you lose everything?" Vilma asked, cautiously curious.

"The war," the guilty man promptly responded. "A battle fought near the plantation, the slaves revolted and left. The harvest was completely lost."

This story was easily acceptable. Similar situations were known to have happened across the South.

"Dexter, a military man is coming!" Vilma said as she spotted a young recruit approaching.

"Private," Dexter called the enlisted man, "come here."

The young man, surprised, stopped close to them.

"This lady needs your help," Dexter said. "She wants to make a formal accusation against this man. Arrest him"

The request was not quite understood. The soldier shook his head, uncertain what to do.

"We want to bring him to the authorities," Dexter explained further, "to file charges."

"Sorry, Sergeant, I know nothing about that," the soldier admitted.

"Help us to find a judicial court, and we will do the rest," Dexter insisted.

"This is my first time in town," the private declared. "I do not know my way around. I'm going back to the barracks right now."

The situation was becoming embarrassing, far from a favorable outcome for Vilma. The young recruit could not help.

"Thank you, soldier." Dexter released him. Turning around, he tried a last recourse. Facing the people still watching, he asked them, "Please, who knows where a court to file charges against someone is?"

Nobody answered. The few remaining standing near them moved away. Dexter was annoyed. Here was the man responsible of causing Vilma so much painful damage but they had no opportunity to punish him. Dexter was saddened that he had failed to give her, if not complete restitution, at least some satisfaction.

"You still possess the plantation, no?" Dexter questioned searching for some positive point to take out of the situation.

"I took a mortgage to expand," the man explained. "Due the war, I missed many payments."

"Transfer the property to Vilma," Dexter interrupted him. "She will drop the charges."

"Sorry, the bank already repossessed it," the thief informed them.

"How do we know you are not lying?" Dexter rebuked him.

"The bank is two blocks up," the trembling man answered, signaling straight ahead. "We can go there."

"This case has no solution!" Dexter dismayed.

If the man was telling the truth, then he had no means to reimburse Vilma. According to his story, life had already treated him hard. Though Vilma wanted this dishonorable man in jail, what benefit would it bring to her? Seeing him in shambles was depressing; punishment comes in different forms.

"In spite of meeting a dishonest person like you," Vilma said, facing the hurtful man, "nowadays I am a very lucky, happy woman. Past troubles no longer spoil my life."

"To hear this gives me some relief," the unworthy man said ceremoniously.

"To get into a legal procedure makes no sense under these circumstances," Vilma realized. "If I file charges and he goes to trial, I must come back. To travel is not secure these days, almost impossible," she conceded.

"What you want to do?" Dexter asked.

"I don't expect to meet him again," Vilma concluded, "and he will leave probably the city as quickly as possible. I'll let him go, but under other conditions, I would not hesitate to prosecute till I see him going to prison."

"Thank you, Miss Mullen!" the pardoned man said. Bending, he tried to kiss Vilma's hand but she hurriedly avoided him hiding arms behind her back. "I'll always be grateful to you, Miss," the man added politely, dismissing her rejection. Not waiting to know if she'd have second thoughts, he left down the street, glancing back at the couple.

Activities inside the Gilbert mansion became daily routine. As customary, Gabriel met with Cecil, answering questions his father had. They started skipping discussion of major problems and bad news from the Confederacy. Gabriel always checked with LaBelle as to the daily treatment of the sick man before leaving to tend the plantation. Wade had orders not to refer problems to Cecil.

LaBelle was dusting Cecil's desk, careful not to displace any papers or objects on it, especially the tray full of the master's medications.

"Miss Anne 'sed' to see her," Clydette, coming in, told LaBelle who continued dusting; such a request sounded out of the ordinary. Miss Anne knew very well Gabriel's instructions about her duties.

"When did she say that?"

"Now, when I was in her room; she said me to tell you," Clydette replied.

LaBelle stopped cleaning. She looked at the patient sitting in the executive chair, reading the *Charleston Mercury* newspaper.

"Clean the sofa," she instructed Clydette, walking out. "Stay here till I come back."

Clydette picked up the cloth LaBelle had left on the desk and did as instructed. Anne complained to LaBelle that a dress she clearly remembered having sent to the laundry was missing. This sort of happening was not rare, but now, due to the special situation with her family, she could not afford to ignore something like that. To request new clothing was not advisable. LaBelle, disturbed, came downstairs and went out to the slaves' quarters.

Cecil Gilbert was rapidly skimming the newspaper pages. The reports were too optimistic, hardly ever agreeing with the news going mouth to mouth in every corner of the South, through towns big and small. Even he, confined in his mansion, knew better than the accounts published. Suddenly, a sharp pain hit his chest. He stopped reading and put the paper down, his head confused and his vision blurred. A second strike hit him. Hurriedly, he motioned his right hand toward the medicine tray on the desk, trying to grasp the one needed, nitroglycerine. His hands shaking out of control pushed the tray, prescription bottles falling to the ground. Short of breath, in pain, he could not speak. He looked around for help. A sound close to growling came out his mouth. Clydette froze. What was that? Frightened, she turned around to see the Master struggling. Trembling, face contracted, Cecil watched in terror Clydette at his side, the only one that could help. He wanted to tell the young slave which medication to pick up, but even if he could talk, it would not be any good since she was illiterate. Eyes wide opened, unable to move, Cecil saw Clydette bending down, searching through the gathered medications. She raised her body, the bottle of nitroglycerine in hands; she took out a tablet and placed it under the tongue of the sick Master with her black fingers.

"Francis, I needed not to ask," James Fitzgerald said, coming to the back terrace, "you are doing better and better." He shook hands with his partner.

"Yes, thank God, he is recovering," Mary Dumont confirmed.

"My daughter has something to do with this, too," the patient added.

"Following doctor's orders made it possible, with God's assistance, of course," Nell completed.

"By the way, how is your husband, Nell?"

"He is fine, James; yesterday I received a letter from him; his father is not doing well; had a heart attack."

"Nell, tell him what happened with the slave," her mother intervened but she was not particularly interested. Then Mary explained the story herself: "When his father had the emergency, a slave whom Nell had taught to write and read was the only one there. Since she could read, was able to find and give him the right medication, saving his life."

Cecil Gilbert's health condition seemed stable after some prescription changes and advice. Still, his past aspect, energy and authoritarian flair did not return. Sitting in a comfortable chair specially adapted for him, he spent hours without saying a word. Nothing was wrong with his vocal cords, according to the doctors; he had simply lost interest. Nothing around him got his attention. Gabriel ordered the servants to rearrange Edna's downstairs apartment for him so he could avoid going up and down stairs; he preferred to stay in the private office during the day.

Gabriel walked into the mansion after a long, tiresome day around the property. The slaves were not as passive, submissive as before. Stopping in the office, he briefly talked to his father, informing him about minor details only, serious problems, out of the question. He checked with LaBelle how the patient had behaved today, and then Gabriel left. As he was going up the semicircular stairs, someone knocked the front door. Curiously, he waited, watching LaBelle coming out of the office to open it. A military man holding hands with a woman came in. Recognizing them immediately, Gabriel froze as the couple, gazing at the opened Cecil's office door, came toward him.

"Of course, you did not expect us," the man, a sergeant, said, walking with the help of a crutch.

"Dexter!"

Gabriel advanced to meet them, but he stopped a few steps from the floor by the icy, defiant tone of his not-long-ago close, dear friend.

"We're just here to tell you we are moving far away," Dexter said angrily, keeping close to his female companion, Vilma. "We will not say where to anybody from Roseville."

The belligerent attitude shocked Gabriel deeply. He couldn't comprehend the animosity his friend displayed and the unthinkable presence of Vilma Mullen.

"No one will hear from us," Dexter continued, excited. "We will not keep contact with or recognize anybody from this town ever again."

What happened? Why was Dexter so angry, vengeful? Gabriel could not fathom a valid answer. He had always treated him as a brother, looked toward his wellbeing. Was war responsible of this complete reversal of feeling? For his hatred?

"We got married in Charleston," Dexter added indicating Vilma, his anger fading a little. "I will defend her against everybody. She did not want to come but she will follow anyplace I go."

The news pleased Gabriel. He wished to congratulate them but it was not appropriate. The tense moment and Dexter's stiff look advised him to stand still. Returning to a resentful tone, Dexter expressed his last, rancorous wish. "I hope we will never meet again." Turning, with the help of Vilma, waiting for nothing else they walked away. Gabriel, standing on the stairs, saw them crossing in front Cecil's office door where an incredulous man, too weak to do anything, watched the couple passing by. LaBelle, eyes wet, opened the front door allowing them to go out.

Gabriel woke up in the middle of the night. He could not sleep in spite of the burden resting on his shoulders. At home he had a sick father who needed attention, the supervision of the plantation and the constant tension war imposed on both owners and slaves. Gabriel counted on little help which mainly came from Wade who Gabriel left without many responsibilities since he no longer trusted him.

Noise coming from outside rushed him to go to the window overlooking the road crossing ahead. The first sun's rays started to brighten a sky still full of stars. Soldiers on horses and on foot went along the way, marching in silence. It was the first time so many military men went through Roseville. Each region kept soldiers for its defense; evidently these men came due to urgent reasons. News of the Union's troops invading nearby states must be true. They needed reinforcements. Then, Gabriel thought, the Confederacy's hopes for victory must be escaping even faster.

Cecil's medications, along with LaBelle's care, were working. He was gaining strength and will. Gabriel did not mention the passing of the soldiers. Cecil retired early that night. Before going to bed himself, Gabriel, following his intuition, checked to make sure the weapons kept in the wooden cabinet in the private office were ready.

Gabriel opened his eyes, jumped from bed and looked down the dusty road. Cavalry soldiers marching, going opposite they went on past nights, dirty, in no formation at all, in clear retreat. The vision was not an encouraging one. Gabriel came back; sat on the bed, worried. Unfortunately, these days hardly anything improved, and hearing positive news was a jolly occurrence. It was always better to prepare for perilous, bad days. Poor Dixie!

A heavy atmosphere covered town and countryside alike. Nobody could explain or deny it, but rumors of fighting nearby arose insistently, some declaring victory for the South and others defeat but no one was able to proof their version. Small numbers of soldiers crossed town, increasing the veracity of both sides. Over the next days, an uneasy calm, no movement in sight. Different accounts of events came out, each source confident of their claims.

The news hit Roseville too often and was difficult to ignore. Reports of pillaging of mansions, businesses, recruits abandoning military service grew at an alarming rate. Whenever group of renegades were seen near an area lacking local authority or military presence, each household became a fortress. When a close case of vandalism reached town, citizens locked their doors and diligently got ready to defend themselves. The Gilbert mansion was no exception. Gabriel prepared the household to face any emergency. He even instructed Anne how to use a rifle, after overcoming her reluctance.

Gabriel finished adding a long list of numbers. The total was much lower than expected. A bad harvest. He put the paper aside and checked over the other documents on the executive desk in his father's office. Finally, he filed them in a drawer, stood, blew out the candle and then walked out of the office. Something made him take a look outside. There, beyond the mansion's fence, a group of men on foot. Gabriel closed the curtains rapidly. From a back door came Wade.

"Gabriel, there are men all around us," he confirmed.

"Yes, I saw them," Gabriel answered. "I think they are renegades. We should have reinforced the locks of the entrance gate."

Both men remained at the window. Gabriel moved the curtain again, gazing outside. The night was clear. "They are looking at the gardens," Gabriel said, letting the hanging cloth fall back. LaBelle, followed by Clydette, came from an interior back room.

"Call Anne," Gabriel told her and went into the office with Wade. LaBelle sent Clydette upstairs. Gabriel and Wade took rifles and ammunitions from the wooden cabinet, carrying them out. Anne and Clydette came down the staircase, their faces worried.

"Anne, LaBelle," Gabriel gave rifles to both women, "go upstairs. Remember, wait for my orders. Clydette will reload the emptied guns."

Carrying the rifles and bullets, the women went upstairs, positioning themselves in different windows.

"Gabriel!" Cecil called, coming out of his bedroom in a wheelchair.

"Keep watching," Gabriel instructed Wade going to his father.

Wade checked outside; some rebels were near the entrance, others walking up and down the fence.

"I can help," Cecil offered.

Gabriel had no time to argue. He pushed his father's wheelchair into the private office and placed him behind a window with a view of the entrance trail. He checked Cecil was properly covered with blankets, seated and motionless.

"Father, wait for my signal. Make the first shots over their heads." Cecil agreed.

Gabriel left the office to join Wade. "What are they doing?" the young man asked, separating the curtain to peek out. He saw a few men coming inside the path to the mansion. He let the curtain down and charged a rifle.

"Anne, LaBelle, open your windows," Gabriel called, unlocking his. Wade got ready.

"Fire!" Gabriel ordered. A simultaneous round of bullets came out of the mansion from upstairs and downstairs.

"Stop!" Gabriel requested. "That was only a warning," he yelled, his head out, addressing the men now standing in the middle of the trail frozen by the unexpected reception. "Next time we'll shoot to kill," he advised with strong voice.

After some hesitation, the unlawful men cautiously advanced toward the mansion. "Fire!" Gabriel commanded. The outlaws, bullets all around, hitting their heels, ran towards the entrance gate, going out, disappearing onto the road.

Dear Nell:

To know your father's health is improving as mention in the long- awaited letter I just received made us very happy. Our congratulations. Unfortunately, I have no good news. My father, not completely recovered from the heart attack, suffered a stroke. His right side is paralyzed. To get medical treatment nowadays is very difficult. Everything around here has changed. The surrender of our troops was too hard for us to accept. We are trying to maintain the mansion straight with no help. Thank God LaBelle is still with us. She takes care of father. The rest, solved as best as possible. Confident are enjoying Mr. Dumont's recovery,

Always yours,

Gabriel

Nell put the letter down. A somber, sad feeling came to her, visualizing Gilbert's mansion at the present time. She felt guilty, should be there to share the uncomfortable days the end of hostilities must have levied on each Southerner, as in the North, the assassination of President Lincoln, a traumatic blow that shocked equally supporters and opponents.

"Nell, what happened?" Mary Dumont asked, coming where she was sitting alone in the terrace, her eyes wet.

"No good news from Roseville, Mother," she answered, gaining composure. "The time has come for me to consider returning."

Mary was surprised. Such an announcement, even though understandable, was not expected.

"The war is over. There is no danger traveling now," Nell continued. "Father is doing well, no doubt he will continue to gain strength and by the time I leave, he will be back to normal."

Nell's voice was so firm, Mrs. Dumont could not find a reasonable argument to delay her daughter's inevitable departure.

Americana

The train engine rode smoothly over the rails at Roseville's station coming to a stop with its bell ringing announcing its arrival. Nell, carrying a small suitcase and a purse, got out of the car. The pedestrians milling around were quite different from those she had witnessed not long ago. Missing were well-dressed ladies and polite people. Today, everybody was in a hurry. A great majority of them black men.

Nell walked gazing around. She saw Gabriel holding the horse's reins in a buggy looking at the train.

"Alone?" Nell asked as she got closer to him.

"Yes, I could not get anyone. How was your trip?"

"Not amusing. All I saw was destruction. My luggage is on the train."

"Please, hold the horse; I'll pick it up. Be careful."

Nell sat on the driver's seat holding the reins; Gabriel went to the train. She knew the place, although it seemed so different. Gabriel came back carrying a big suitcase, followed by a black man with another trunk. They stored them in back of the vehicle. Gabriel paid the man. Taking control, Gabriel put the carriage in motion. He asked about her father.

"He is fine. These last weeks his health improved satisfactorily. And Mr. Gilbert?"

"Stable. He has responded well but slow to medications."

"He will recover."

"We're not sure, Nell. He is not the same; he's too quiet, hardly talks."

"That is understandable. I mean, after being seriously ill, people change. My father did."

"Maybe. But knowing him, it is difficult to adapt and accept his new personality."

"Give him time, Gabriel. The old Mr. Gilbert will come back."

"I hope you are right, Nell."

The buggy left the last houses of the town behind; green vegetation was now everywhere. "Thank God the countryside here did not change much," Nell commented remembering the past. "Gabriel, as you solicited, I brought currency from the

European clients Mr. Gilbert requested to be sent to my father's office."

"Great. That will help a lot," Gabriel said. "Father was right to have payments made up there."

"My father's partner, Mr. Fitzgerald, will advise if he receives more funds."

Gabriel thought for a moment. "I doubt it. We have not delivered cotton to Europe for a long time," he explained.

Nell nodded acknowledgment. "You said the mansion has no helpers?"

"Nell, dear, today it is not the place you knew." Gabriel sighed. "We are lucky LaBelle is with us. The rest of the slaves, well, now are free had left the crops. They still live there, but no one works for us."

"I know slavery was abolished, but what do they do now?"

"You saw them in town. All day they're going around, doing petty jobs."

"Who is working in the fields?"

"Nobody, Nell. Suddenly to pick cotton is wrong, evil."

"It happened too fast. To be free is new for them. Things will return to normalcy."

"I hope so."

"Changes always cause distrust. In the end, order will prevail."

"That will take a long, painful time, I fear. Nobody was prepared for this."

"True. In a few months, things will settle down," Nell continued, still optimistic. "Washington is helping, no?"

"Yes. Northerners who we call 'carpetbaggers' are implementing military reconstruction laws. If helped by a Southerner, he will be named a 'scalawag.'"

"That does not help either side. People must agree with the new status. There is no going back."

"I know, you cannot imagine how hard it is for us," Gabriel conceded. The buggy hit a hole, shaking its passengers.

"How is Anne . . . Aunt Mabel?" Nell asked changing the subject.

"Fine; they are waiting at the mansion. Aunt Mabel and LaBelle made father regain some life back in his body."

"Clydette does not help?"

"Oh, Nell, she and Wade, as the saying goes the first rats to abandon ship at the first sign of water! They left as soon as we lost authority."

At the entrance of the Gilbert's estate, Gabriel, slowing the horse's trot, guided the carriage to a stop at the main entrance. He got out, helped Nell off and opened the mansion's front door.

They walked into the entrance hall. Aunt Mabel came out of Cecil's office. With arms opened wide, she embraced Nell.

"Oh, my dear, so glad to see you back!"

Nell could not answer. A sudden wave of emotions made her to freeze. Holding tight, both women caressed each other. Gabriel at a distance watched them.

"Had a good trip, Nell?"

"Yes, Aunt Mabel."

"How is the family, your father?"

"Well, thanks God. I heard Mr. Gilbert had a stroke."

"He is going to overcome it. Come, see him." Holding hands, they walked toward the office. "Oh dear, so many events around Roseville to catch up." Aunt Mabel explained with friendly, natural tone. "Darlene's family sold their plantation and moved out; Dexter married Vilma Mullens, the nurse who took care of him and saved his leg from amputation. I don't know if you are aware of this but better sooner than later; anyway, this is something belonging to the past. He decided to move out and did not tell where even to his parents."

Nell did not say a word. Getting to the office Aunt Mabel pulled the door open. Both women went inside while Gabriel stayed out handling the luggage.

"Nell, let me advise him."

There, at the side of the executive desk in a wheelchair was the Master, covered with blankets and pillows behind his head. He was quiet, semi-sleeping. Standing near him was LaBelle.

"Miss Nell!"

The loyal servant could not hold her joy.

"How are you LaBelle?" Nell came and put both arms around her shoulders, embarrassing her, not accustomed to such friendly behavior.

Cecil Gilbert opened his eyes at hearing noises.

"Look who is back," Aunt Mabel embracing Nell told him.

He raised his head and took a quick examination at the smiling faces looking at him. Slowly, he put his head down, returning to the passiveness that now rules his days and character.

"No talking today," the good Aunt said. "Perhaps tomorrow."

Grabbing Nell by an arm, she guided her out of the office, joining Gabriel who was coming down the stairs.

"Where is Anne?" Nell questioned.

"She is up in her rooms," Gabriel answered.

"I want to see her."

They went upstairs. Anne's door was ajar. Gabriel pushed it open. Anne was sitting facing the window. She turned showing her pale face and sad expression. Nell advanced straight and Anne jumped off the couch and ran to her, joining in a tight, emotional embrace. Tears streamed profusely, their bodies shaking.

"Nell, Anson is dead!"

"I know, Anne. I am so sorry."

At a distance, Gabriel and Aunt Mabel speechless watched the young women. Afterward, Gabriel escorted Nell to their apartments.

"I am very tired," Nell said.

"Go to bed. Nobody will disturb you," Gabriel told her. "LaBelle will unpack the luggage later," he added as he picked up some of his clothes left in the parlor as he walked out the room, closing the door.

That evening LaBelle, smiling and happy, put a big, steaming pot of stew on the table. Evidently, she was very pleased to have a new member at the dinner table.

"Sorry, Miss Nell," she explained. "I could not get anything better. The kitchen's shelves are almost empty."

"She understands, LaBelle," Aunt Mabel replied, taking care of serving the food. LaBelle left. The meal at the Gilberts' was not as usual. Today no fancy, extra dishes. It was a sober table.

"Is it difficult to get supplies?" Nell asked.

"There are no personnel working in the country," Gabriel stated.

"I remember Mr. Gilbert ordered to grow vegetables in the plantation," Nell said.

"This is some of the food we are eating today," Aunt Mabel said. "LaBelle gets whatever she can find in town. Gabriel picks up vegetables and fruits from the fields."

"The land needs attention. The tobacco crop is already lost," Gabriel added.

"Farm workers are needed," Nell said.

"That would help, if anyone is willing to do it," Gabriel pointed out.

"But people need to work in order to earn a living," Nell reasoned.

"That is not understood yet," Gabriel answered.

"I suppose will take time to adapt to the new working rules," Nell expressed thoughtfully.

"Slavery is still too close to peoples' minds. Changes are difficult to implement," Gabriel added.

"My husband was right when he freed his slaves' years ago," Aunt Mabel commented.

They finished their dinner in silence. As was customary, they went to the parlor. LaBelle brought fruits and tea, and then she left. Aunt Mabel served tea. Nell sat close to her, Gabriel standing facing them.

"And about LaBelle, what is her position now?"

"Oh, she is so good, Nell," Aunt Mabel answered. "We ask for nothing but it is not necessary. She cooks, cleans and helps with Cecil."

"As far as she wants to stay, we'll keep her," Gabriel assured.

"She is afraid to go outside," Aunt Mabel continued. "She did not leave the mansion when the others did and now they are angry about her."

"Nobody is going to hurt LaBelle," Gabriel affirmed.

"Anne, does she not help?" Nell questioned.

"Oh, dear, she promised to clean her rooms and she does but we have seen LaBelle coming out of her apartment too, and that is all."

"I hope this situation will stop," Gabriel interrupted in a soft, low tone. "She has shown her frustration long enough. To prolong it will damage her and the rest of us."

"My dear Gabriel," Aunt Mabel said as she turned facing her nephew, "I pray for that to happen. After Cecil had the stroke, I spoke to her. She insisted he was already dead. I am afraid it will take her a long, long time to get over that."

"Is not her position against Mr. Gilbert too tough?" Nell asked.

"Dear, she blames him for nothing less than Anson's death," Aunt Mabel responded.

"I should have used my authority" Gabriel lamented, "at the beginning of this problem. But I could not obligate anyone to do my will. Now it is late."

Back at their apartments, Nell and Gabriel walked into the small entrance parlor.

"Where's your furniture, bed?" Nell inquired.

"I moved into the main bedroom when you left. I did not know when you'd be back," Gabriel explained.

"I see." Nell said walking a few steps into the main room. All was in order. Luggage, emptied. Evidently, LaBelle had been there.

"Sorry; I will sleep in father's room," Gabriel proposed. "He lives now downstairs."

"That is not necessary ... there's enough room here," Nell decided.

Never had so few words produced greater joy in a single soul.

Tenderly, he came closer, embraced and kissed her.

Roseville was crowded, although the make-up of the pedestrian traffic was quite different. Holding hands, Nell and Gabriel walked past the old familiar stores, now with more popular announcement signs.

"Mr. and Mrs. Gilbert!" M. Pierre, the old proprietor standing at the entrance of his boutique saluted them; foreign accent less noticeable.

"Monsieur Pierre," Gabriel responded stopping.

Smiling, the man made a slight reverence. "This is a pleasant surprise."

"Dear, you remember Monsieur Pierre?"

"Yes, Aunt Mabel and I frequently visited his store."

"Glad to see old friends in town," Monsieur Pierre politely said. "An elegant hat, Madame."

"Thanks, Mr. Pierre."

"Unfortunately, it's not from my boutique."

"I bought it in Boston," Nell informed.

"Ah, it is a great city!" Mr. Pierre said. "Please come in." He said signaling inside.

"We are not shopping today, Monsieur Pierre," Gabriel explained. "I am looking for people wanting to work in my plantation."

Mr. Pierre's face changed; he realized this was not a sales opportunity. Anyway, they were potential customers and doing them a service today may repay tomorrow. "Mr. Gilbert, check the meeting house," he advised.

"Thank you, Monsieur Pierre."

"Glad to help anytime," the store owner replied. "Always at your service." Smiling, with a bow, he saw them off, walking down the walkway.

"You still call him *monsieur*?" Nell asked.

"That is how we always did."

"He is as American as we are, Gabriel."

"True, love; however, everybody appreciates a gallant remark."

The historic, ample hall so often used as the voice of the ruling slaveholders was crowded but with completely different personalities than in the past. A great majority of those there were black men and women. Gabriel and Nell advanced through the central aisle holding hands, examining the people in assembly at both sides. At a group, Gabriel recognized some faces. Coming closer, he came to view the back of a white man talking to them. His figure was familiar. Soon, Gabriel identified him. It was Wade, who guessed the presence of someone well-known when the ex-slaves nervously moved back at the advance of the incoming couple. Turning, he faced them.

"Mr. Gabriel Gilbert and Mrs." Wade said smiling and offering his right hand.

"I thought you had left town," Gabriel said coldly, holding his hands at his back and gazing around.

"I just came back to do business," Wade answered, putting his hands into his trousers' pockets.

From behind the ex-slaves, who kept themselves away from Gabriel, came a woman wearing a vividly colored dress, makeup, earrings, a big hat with long, bright feathers, her arms covered with bracelets. She came to a stop close to Wade.

"Miss Nell!" the woman greeted with chilly, unpleasant voice. Gabriel looked curiously, wondering who she was. Nell had no problem identifying the person under such apparel: "Clydette," she saluted back.

"I didn't expect to see you here," the ex-servant said moving her head, making the feathers to dance.

"If you are looking for workers," Wade intervened signaling to the group behind him, "they are ready for employment."

"Many of them, if I recall right, worked for me. I will hire anyone wanting to go back."

"Not me," Clydette clarified. "I'm now a singer."

Nell and Gabriel held their shock at an involuntary reaction of disbelief.

"Wade is getting places for me in Charleston, Savannah, and Augusta," she claimed going back to the other ex-slaves.

"I will send to your estate the people you'd request for work," Wade informed. "They are under my orders. You pay me."

"No," Gabriel said, getting impatient. "I will hire and pay directly to the workers."

"They will go when and where I say," Wade insisted.

"I will not hire through intermediaries," Gabriel said firmly, "nor help anybody taking advantage of them."

"They are free people," Nell reminded Wade, "can do whatever they want."

"Listen," Gabriel said, advancing toward the shy group, "you need nobody to find work. I will employ and pay directly anyone who goes back to my plantation."

Silence. Eyes downcast, nobody moved. The ex-Master's presence still affected the former slaves. Wade walked around watching the indecisive people attentively. No one dared to respond or even look at their previous Master. Bondage was still too fresh. Smiling, Wade walked around the undecided group. Disappointed, the Gilberts left. There was nothing they could do.

Gabriel came from the fields and walked into the private office. Cecil, in his wheelchair, was quiet. Aunt Mabel was at his side sitting in a rocking chair.

"How is he?"

"The same, Gabriel. He had his medications and will take the last ones after dinner," Aunt Mabel answered. "Sit, nephew. You look tired." He sat on the executive chair behind the fancy desk. Nell came in.

"Anybody showed up?" she asked approaching her husband.

"Nobody. The plantation is deserted and the cotton is ripening."

Nell got closer. Taking his hands she stood at his side.

"LaBelle is emptying the buggy," he reported. "I found two chickens, eggs, and vegetables."

"Good. That will help," Nell responded.

"I see no alternative but to get workers through Wade," Gabriel conceded.

"Never. That will put us under his command. There must be another way."

Cecil raised his head and looked around, stopping his gaze at each face. Then he lowered the chin to his chest.

"I need to go home," Aunt Mabel said.

"Yes," Gabriel agreed, "you have been with us long enough. When the buggy is emptied, I will drive you there, Aunt."

At dinner, Nell instructed LaBelle to bring Cecil to the dining room. Once everybody was there, the domestic servant brought the food. Nell started serving.

"Miss Nell, I will feed Master Gilbert later," LaBelle requested. "I need to carry up Anne's supper."

"Just a moment." Nell stopped serving the food, realizing that changes were necessary. "This must end. Aunt Mabel went home; you are covering enough responsibilities. No more food deliveries."

"Miss Nell, no dinner for her?"

"Oh, yes."

"Miss Anne has no food to eat if I . . . "

"LaBelle, stay here. I am going to talk to her." Nell left the dining room and went straight to Anne's apartment.

"I regret to inform you that LaBelle can no longer bring up dinner. She already has enough household chores that she does out of the kindness of her heart. Therefore, I suggest Anne that you come down."

Nell did not wait for an answer, immediately left the room. Downstairs, she joined Gabriel and his father at the table. LaBelle, worried, was feeding Cecil.

"Miss Nell, I can do it." She insisted.

"LaBelle, you will not," Nell ordered firmly.

The noises of spoons and forks were the only sounds heard. Cecil's passiveness seemed transmitted to the rest gathering there. A shadow at the entrance caused everybody to stop eating. It was Anne. She quietly reached the table and sat down. Nell and

Gabriel continued their meal. Anne served herself and started eating. Cecil Gilbert opened his eyes and mouth that LaBelle promptly filled with food avoiding any sound to come out. Anne did not look at her father. It was a quiet reunion.

LaBelle administered Cecil's medication and Gabriel pushed the sick master's wheelchair to his rooms. Nell started picking up the tableware. Anne stood ready to leave, but instead, holding herself she picked-up, carried dishes and glassware to the kitchen.

"Thanks, Anne."

"Are you doing the dishes, Nell?"

"No, I'm going to take care of Mr. Gilbert. Aunt Mabel went home. LaBelle will come. She handles the kitchen better and faster than I."

Anne felt sad, unsettled, not knowing why she came down breaking her long-held vows. Silently she went stairs up and Nell to Cecil's room.

The situation at the plantation did not improve. Gabriel was deeply disappointed with the lack of workers to pick up cotton, a crucial task. On one occasion, when he was collecting vegetables, he saw ex-slaves in the proximity. But they ran at the sight of the old master, evidently still afraid of the ex-owner. He did not try to stop them. The only good news in those gloomy days was edible supplies improved in town stores, bringing relief to the menu at the Gilbert's mansion.

Time was running out for cotton picking, which required experienced workers. Gabriel did not mention again employing through Wade, even though the necessity for workers was evident. Nell was aware of the urgency. As a desperate recourse, she proposed one night at bedtime that they use all hands available.

"What do you mean?" Gabriel asked.

"You, me and LaBelle."

"We, picking cotton?"

"Why not? That is better than doing nothing," Nell said.

Gabriel did not argue. Anyway, working in the fields would dissipate the frustration of being idle but . . .

"Who is going to take care of Father?" Gabriel inquired.

"I thought about that. Go to Aunt Mabel's residence; ask if she can accompany Mr. Gilbert during the daytime. We will drive her back every afternoon, or she can stay here."

"No doubt she'll come but love; we'll not collect enough cotton for a sale."

"You have clients, no?" Nell asked.

"Yes; they are waiting for an embarkation."

"Gabriel Gilbert, I assure you tonight that we will send them cotton bales soon."

The man smiled at his wife's confidence, wishing to share it. Nell moved toward the night table and blew out the candle. She was not sleepy but unsure to prove her idea.

The next morning, Gabriel picked up Aunt Mabel and drove her to the mansion. Nell had already spoken to LaBelle. The loyal servant did not refuse; she pointed out her long disconnection with cotton picking but ready to do her new assignment.

Nell went upstairs to Anne's apartment to attempt the hardest part. The young girl was combing her hair, standing at a mirror.

"Glad to see you are taking care of yourself," Nell congratulated her sister-in-law.

"I do not know how long it has been since I did it," Anne answered putting the comb on the table.

Nell stood close to her. "Anne, when coming downstairs you heard Gabriel describing the condition of the plantation due the lack of workers," she started calmly, with the most natural tone she could muster. "I gave your brother currencies collected by my father from Mr. Gilbert's overseas clients. He had requested that money to be held safely in the North. So far, Gabriel has managed to cover expenses. But for how long with that he will be able to support the family, I do not know. Here at home, one person needs special attention and his health comes first. In short, the plantation must produce again. There are no longer slaves; so far, no workers have appeared. Gabriel, with my help and LaBelle joining us, we expect will pick up enough cotton in a reasonable amount of time to do a sale." She stopped, trying to think of favorable arguments to consolidate her plea.

"Nell, honestly, I am not interested in those problems," Anne frankly stated.

"Eventually this will affect every member of the family," Nell said more directly.

"The plantation can be sold," Anne suggested.

"Gabriel does not want," Nell rebutted. "On the contrary, he is trying to save this land. Anyway, that would be a terrible mistake at today's economic conditions."

Nell pacing slowly, looking out the window at the surrounding forest came back to the original subject. "My intention is to make everyone aware of the crisis. No doubt this concerns each one of us. We could not get workers. Wade seemed to have control of the ex-slaves with experience in cotton picking. Gabriel, LaBelle and I will do it. We could use an extra hand. I am asking for your help."

She kept watching the outside, waiting, uncertain about the effectiveness of her words. Anne looked at her with curiosity, not completely sure if she had heard right.

"Are you talking seriously? I, picking cotton?"

"My father says: 'There are no good or bad occupations but simply occupations.'"

"I will never descend to a slave position," the girl said fiercely.

"Slavery is gone, Anne. To do it does not make anybody better or worse. Our future depends on it."

"Always should be slaves. This war brought nothing but misfortune, painful days."

"And liberty," Nell added.

"Slaves had food and shelter. They owed us everything; we owe them nothing," Anne countered.

"Gabriel told me a slave woman nursed you when you were a baby and got sick and your mother could not, helping you to get well, taking care of you for years."

Anne did not answer, her eyes fixed to the ground. Inside her, something came up: memories of childhood, a lovely black woman holding and caressing her.

"Anyway," Nell added a final thought, "this will probe how worthy we are. It is for our welfare. If everybody in this household is doing it, I see no reason why you should not when the benefits will reach you."

Nell came downstairs. Upon getting to the first floor, LaBelle gave her a long sack, which she put over her shoulders. Gabriel had already one. Aunt Mabel from the open office door waved them on their way out to 'slave' work.

The noise of steps coming from the stairs stopped them. All eyes went to the circular staircase. Anne was hurrying down.

"Wait for me," she requested descending the last steps.

LaBelle came to Anne, offering her a long sack and helped to fit it around her shoulders. Then they continued outside under the wet eyes and blessing from the good Aunt and got into the buggy. Gabriel repeatedly shook the animal's reins, hurrying the horse. Nell held hard. Anne, at her side, grabbed the buggy's seat end to keep from falling during the fast, shaking ride. LaBelle sitting in the back, wondering why the urgency. Nobody was waiting for them, for goodness sake!

At the cotton field, LaBelle, in charge of training Nell went to parallel aisles; Gabriel and Anne to the next. "Anne, when the bolls turn brown, they open," Gabriel explained. "They are ripening, showing the soft, white fibers. Pick the seeds from them. If a boll is not opened, keep going to the next plant."

Just like that, they went to work.

Soon the daily work in the cotton field showed it fruits. The amount collected started to add up, making the effort visible and bringing hope, at least to Anne and Nell. Gabriel, knowing the amount needed for a shipment, was less enthusiastic. To reach the required level for a sale was far away from them but he kept his thoughts to himself.

Back at the mansion, Aunt Mabel had news for them. "Mr. Greenfield was here."

"Who?" Nell questioned.

"An old family friend," Gabriel explained. "Surely you saw him often."

"Dexter's father," Anne said to complete the visitor's identification.

"Well," Aunt Mabel said, ignoring the interruption, "he talked to Cecil for an hour. Cecil listened attentively, answering at times with short words."

"That is really good news," Gabriel said.

"Have they heard from Dexter?" Anne asked.

"Mr. Greenfield is very sad," Aunt Mabel replied. "He is selling his plantation and leaving Roseville. Dexter wrote and told him not to mention where they are moving to anybody."

No one ventured to ask more. "Oh, another thing," Aunt Mabel added, "A doctor opened an office in town. He comes from Atlanta. He left because many families moved away due to the war's destruction; he likes Roseville."

"This is the best thing to happen to this town lately," Gabriel pointed out. "I will visit and ask him to take care of Father."

That night at dinner, they occupied all the seats at the table. Aunt Mabel joined them. LaBelle brought food with her natural promptness, though she showed signs of nervousness and strained gestures. She sat next to Mr. Gilbert, served his special menu and fed him. The spoon fell from her hand.

"LaBelle, are you feeling well?"

"Yes, Miss Nell."

"No, you are not. Tell me what it is."

LaBelle picked up the spoon from the floor and went to the kitchen. Moments later she came back and sat next to the patient and continued to feed him. "C'mon Master Gilbert. Open wide your mouth."

"LaBelle, I have often said, you no longer need to call him 'master'. Mr. Gilbert is right."

"I know, Young Gabriel. I can't do it yet."

"Try," Gabriel insisted. "After all, you must start some day."

"I will, Young Gabriel."

"Anyway, LaBelle why are you so nervous?"

"Who, me, Miss Nell?"

"Mrs. Nell," she corrected. "Yes, it is clear something is bothering you."

"Sorry," LaBelle finally admitted. "Today when I went to Roseville to buy food, on a placard of those recently opened speakeasy saloons, I saw they were advertising Clydette."

"Really?" The news surprised Anne.

"She said is a singer now," Nell reminded.

"If my poor cousin could see her daughter in that place, she'd die again," LaBelle affirmed.

"My goodness, this town is advancing at high speed," Aunt Mabel commented. "We have a doctor, entertainment, what is next?"

"Gabriel, when is the doctor coming?" Nell asked.

"Dr. Wolfe, that's his name, will be here tomorrow afternoon. Therefore, we will have a short working day since I want to be present when he visits Father."

"I can stay picking cotton with LaBelle," Anne volunteered.

"That is not a good idea, Anne. It would be better to come back home. You know, I carry a rifle to the fields; so far, we had no problems, but I will not leave two women alone, even if armed."

Anne did not argue. Gabriel had respected her obduracy toward Cecil. Anyway, he was now *de facto* head of the family.

"Gabriel," Nell said, stepping in to avoid possible escalation of the topic, "do you have any plan for the Spanish moss cottage?"

Aunt Mabel held her breath. LaBelle looked at Nell holding the spoon in the air.

"No, love. Why?"

"Roseville is growing in many areas but a church is missing."

"What?" Anne was surprised.

"Yes, Gabriel can donate that property to the Catholic Church."

"Good idea, Nell," Anne approved.

"No objection," Gabriel replied. "But Father is the owner. If he agrees, I will initiate the procedures."

Cecil raised his head and gazed around. He seemed was going to speak but instead he remained silent.

Nell was struck with inspiration. "Mr. Gilbert can offer it in memory of Edna, his deceased wife."

Everyone approved the idea.

Gabriel kept close to Anne while picking cotton, watching also Nell and LaBelle not far away. The sun was high, hot. The countryside was green and peaceful. After a while, Gabriel walked toward the buggy parked under a tree and drank water.

Nell came to him. "Gabriel, there is a man with LaBelle," she said, pointing to the cotton field. Gabriel picked up the rifle from the carriage and walked toward them quickly. An old black man was talking to LaBelle. When he saw Gabriel coming, he started moving away.

"C'mon, don't run," LaBelle said, holding him by an arm. "He'll not hurt you."

The man, almost trembling, looked up and down, stayed at her side.

"Young Gabriel," LaBelle said, "here is Mellian. Remember him?"

"Of course," Gabriel answered, hanging the rifle on his shoulder, pushing it back out of view.

"I told him you need people picking cotton."

"Yes, he is one of the best we had in the plantation."

"Well," LaBelle, turning to the black man, pressured, "'what you say?"

The old man lowered his head, too nervous to face his previous master.

"Nothing to be afraid of," Gabriel assured him. "You are welcome. I will employ anyone wanting to come back."

"I told him," LaBelle affirmed.

Smiling, looking at Gabriel, the man finally gathered the courage to speak. "Lemme sed wid my fambly." He then left as fast as he could, amazed he had spoken directly to the old master's son.

The new doctor arrived at the mansion. Gabriel and family were expecting him. After the formal introduction, he went into Cecil's room, escorted by Gabriel, Nell, Aunt Mabel and LaBelle. Later, everyone but LaBelle came back out.

"Continue with the medications," Dr. Wolfe instructed. "This new prescription he should take one a day. If there's any change in his condition, tell me. I will visit him every week. As I told you, when he wants something, make him to speak. No more pointing with his fingers. He can talk."

"Yes, doctor," Aunt Mabel agreed.

"Thanks, Dr. Wolfe," Gabriel said accompanying him to the main door. "We will do exactly as you ordered."

In the fields, Gabriel did not wish to spoil the good, hard work, faith and enthusiasm shown by Nell and company. Anyway, a few sacks full of cotton already lay on the trails. Gabriel transferred the horse from the buggy to a wagon helped by Nell and they put the sacks into it.

"Thanks, love. I will bring them to the warehouse."

"Let me go, too! I want to see the ginning machine." As said, she jumped into the wagon. Both traveled the short distance to the big house used to process the collected cotton.

"That next building, what is it?" Nell asked curiously as they reached the wooden structure.

"Runaway slaves were kept there for weeks or months as punishment," Gabriel explained as he got off the wagon and opened the door of the warehouse.

Nell made an unpleasant face. "You should tear that building down," she suggested.

Back in the cotton fields, LaBelle was waiting for them. "Good news!" she announced with a big smile.

Gabriel tied the horse to the tree under which the buggy was and helped Nell get out the wagon. He came closer to the maidservant. From the plants in bloom emerged the ex-slave Mellian.

"He came to help us," LaBelle explained.

"So glad to see you back!" Gabriel said with sincere, friendly voice.

"Two young men came with him," LaBelle continued, "and want also to pick up cotton."

"All are welcome," Gabriel affirmed, looking toward the place where LaBelle signaled.

"We want do 'bizness wid Mast . . . Gi'bert'," Mellian said with a broad smile.

"Of course," Gabriel answered promptly. "I will accept anyone."

The presence of ex-slaves gave a different tone to the cotton picking. Nell, who had been waiting for something to happen without knowing exactly what, at last saw a change, a sign that elevated their morale. At the end of the working day, more full sacks were laid down the trail.

Gabriel called Mellian and the others. "That's enough for today," he said but the men could not believe it.

"No, 'lemme do mo'," Mellian said.

But Gabriel rejected him. "Work time is over," the owner explained. "We are leaving, and so you are. I'll pay for your work."

Mellian and friends, eyes wide open, put their hands out to receive the currency, amazed and unaccustomed to be paid. With bright, happy faces, shaking their heads, they thanked the young man. Walking fast at first and then running they disappeared through the cotton fields. They couldn't believe the incredible fact that they had been paid, going home while the sun was still shinning. It was unthinkable to them, a miracle.

The next day when Gabriel and company reached the field, Mellian and even more men were already there. They welcomed the new workers, providing them long sacks and before Gabriel had a chance to say anything, the ex-slaves started picking seed cotton. Now Gabriel knew they would reach the amount needed for a sale, something Nell had never doubted.

The sun was radiant, not a cloud in the sky. Nell, Anne, and Gabriel came to the buggy to drink water.

"If these men are working, I see no need for us to be in the fields," Anne commented.

"I agree," Nell said, "every day more men are joining us but it is too early to leave all the work to them. We should continue till they regularly show up."

Gabriel did not participate in their conversation; both women were right but he did not want to take sides. Finishing refreshing themselves, they returned to laboring.

The trot of a horse coming made many workers to raise their heads. Soon, the rider was visible. It was Wade. Gabriel came out to the road and faced him.

"These men," Wade informed, "are under my orders. I have not authorized them to work at this plantation."

"They came freely," Gabriel responded.

Wade pulled the reins, trotting the horse in circles, ultimately stopping close to Gabriel. "They signed a contract and therefore are illegally here."

"You know very well," Gabriel answered, "they cannot read or write."

"I have papers," Wade insisted, his tone menacing, "signed with an X."

Nell came out of the fields, walked to the buggy, picked up the rifle.

"Nobody is forcing them," Gabriel said, "and they will continue working here if they want."

"Then, I will collect their wages," Wade insisted.

"I pay them directly," Gabriel clearly stated. "If coerced or harassed in any form, I will defend them. Any document could be rescinded, made void. If necessary, I'll challenge its validity in court."

Nell reached Gabriel, the rifle held firmly, her finger on the trigger. Wade at the saddle was visibly angry. Pulling the reins he moved the horse around.

Lacking bargaining strength, the rider proposed, "We must get an agreement." His tone now seemed conciliatory; he knew the young man's steady character very well. Besides, Nell holding a rifle was a dangerous omen.

"There is nothing to negotiate," Gabriel stated. "These are free men; therefore, they can choose where to work."

He said this loud and clear. The laborers had gathered at a distance, watching the men who not long ago were close allies, today battling over them, one clearly on their side.

"We must resolve this," Wade insisted. "We should talk." He kept the horse moving constantly, showing a nervous disposition.

"There's nothing to discuss," Gabriel said. "This meeting is over. You are not welcome. Get out of my property right now."

Nell made more visible the rifle in her hands. Wade knew Gabriel meant every word. Hurriedly, he pulled on the reins and directed the horse's trot to the trail conducting out of Gilbert's realm. Smiling, with a relieved sensation, the ex-slaves returned to work, confident they had security and support in consolidating their new status.

The tension between the Gilberts and the former slaves that existed at the beginning gradually disappeared. Soon women joined the workers, sometimes singing gospels, old forgotten tunes carried deep. The amount of cotton collected grew rapidly due the steady number of experienced men and women now in the fields. Gabriel, with help from Mellian and assistants, hauled sacks to the cotton gin, where the seeds were separated from the cotton fibers, cleaned, dried, pressed into bales, making them smaller, more solid and ready for shipment.

Gradually, life returned to normalcy. The mansion recovered the serenity and castle-like security of old times. Anne and LaBelle sometimes skipped coming to the cotton fields when chores at the mansion demanded their presence. Aunt Mabel continued to be a valuable help. Cecil Gilbert' health improved day by day. Cotton bales started to pile higher and higher, making everybody happy, especially Gabriel. They were getting very near the amount needed to make an overseas shipment profitable.

Nevertheless, diversification of crops was on his mind. He had already discussed it with Mellian, today his most trusted helper. Any doubts felt at first had already vanished. Wade never returned and Gabriel proved to be a lenient, understanding owner.

Working together consolidated the relationship between the old owners and the hired laborers. Earning an income gave the ex-slaves control of their lives and hope in the promising future. Slowly, the old, dreaded label of "master" was staying behind. Men and women came to the cotton fields with a smile on their faces.

Anne came to the supply wagon. She got a drink of water raising a well-worn cup to her lips and refreshing her throat as she gazed at the beautiful view of the trees lining the road that connected the cotton fields. Far in the distance, a military horseman was coming. She held her breath. In her mind, she experienced a flash of past dreams, seeming to recognize the beloved image of Anson as a young valiant knight coming to her rescue. Back to real life, she shook her head, turned it away and stopped such nonsense thoughts. It was actually a Northern military man. The cotton workers noticed him and alerted Gabriel, who walked forward to receive him. The officer reached them.

"My name is Gabriel Gilbert; I'm the owner," he introducing himself coming to the rider.

"Glad to meet you, Mr. Gilbert. I'm Captain O'Neil, in charge of this territory."

Both men shook hands. Nell, Mellian, and other workers stood timidly near Gabriel who presented Nell to the captain. She mentioned was a Northerner. Anne kept hiding behind the wagon, looking and listening to the exchange of words between Gabriel and the military man. Captain O'Neil wanted to know the situation with the laborers, asking Mellian also, once Gabriel introduced him. To the officer's surprise, there no conflicts. The ex-slaves praised their new working conditions, affirming that they had no complaints, even when the new authority pressed them not to hold anything.

LaBelle joined Anne. She knew the young girl was not well but still she did not ask her what was wrong. Instead, she simply placed utensils that had been put away carelessly in their proper order in the wagon.

The visitor, his horse constantly moving, saw Anne. He questioned about her presence; a white young woman in the cotton field was not expected. Nell called and introduced Anne. The officer militarily saluted her. Nell invited him to visit them at the mansion; Gabriel supported the suggestion. The captain said he'd consider it and since everything seemed in order, he left hurriedly toward the road. From behind the trees and bushes, soldiers on horses came out, trotting behind their commander as they left. Gabriel smiled; it was unusual for an officer to be alone. Mellian and the workers went back to cotton picking.

Nell and Anne walked close to Gabriel on their way back to work. "I'm afraid he'll return asking more questions," Nell said.

"That is his job; the war is over," Gabriel answered.

"Will this officer come to visit us?" worried, Anne asked her sister-in-law.

"Probably. Northern men are sociable people." Nell responded.

"My God, I don't have a decent dress to wear."

"Anne, don't worry; I will take care of that."

After many weeks in the fields, nobody was picking cotton. The men and women were too excited. All the wagons at hand, any kind of carriage big enough to carry bales were stationed at the cotton gin warehouse. Gabriel, helped by men and women, were loading the wagons. At last they were ready to make a delivery to Boston for shipping to European clients. The excitement was bigger than the heat, the sweat and the heavy burden of handling the bales. There was no time to lose. Finishing loading, Gabriel took control of the first vehicle, followed by other wagons and guided it to the road leading to town under the happy cheers, enthusiastic singing and hand clapping of those running alongside the heavy cargo bound for the railroad station in Roseville.

Clydette singing career was short, at least in Roseville. Her name soon disappeared from local placards.

Nell stopped working. A discomfort ran through her body. Leaving the long sack on the ground, she went to the supply wagon under a shade tree. Sitting down she took a pitcher and drank a few sips of water. The uncomfortable feeling remained.

Gabriel came. "Tired?" he asked, lifting a water jug.

"It must be the heat," Nell replied, "even though today it is not too hot."

She stood up. Losing her balance, she grabbed her husband's arm.

"Love, what happened?"

"I don't know," she said visibly indisposed. "Lately, I'm not feeling well."

LaBelle came to the wagon. Seeing the pale faces was enough for her. "Come," she said, taking Nell's hands and guiding her to sit down. "What is the problem?"

"Rare sensations. I don't feel in good health, something rare inside. I get hungry at times, and later, an upset stomach."

The symptoms she described were of an indisputable nature.

"Miss Nell, are you going to have a baby?"

Silence. The news, so unexpected, made the couple freeze.

"LaBelle, don't say that."

"Well, Miss Nell, I can tell you right now," the loyal servant said. "Lie down, please."

A few curious men and women gathered close to them. LaBelle passed her hands softly over the young lady's belly then put her ear on the womb, listening carefully. The women watching LaBelle nodded as approving the procedure. LaBelle raised herself and helped Nell to sit straight.

"Miss Nell, surely you are expecting!"

Excitement seemed to overrun everyone. Gabriel embraced and kissed his wife. Noticing the gathering, Anne came over just in time to hear the good news. Happy, she congratulated the lucky parents to be.

"A new Gilbert," Gabriel said. "Thank you! I am the happiest man on earth!"

LaBelle and the people gathered around went back to the fields, commenting the happy news.

"Another Gilbert," Anne said. "Father will be a grandfather."

Gabriel and Nell amazed looked at her. This was the first time she had mentioned "Father" in a long, long time. Rapidly Anne left. Gabriel put his arms around Nell's shoulders reclining his head on hers, deeply, completely happy for the first time in many, many years. From the fields came the singing of the laborers:

"Alleluia . . . Come to me, 0h Lord . . . Come to me!"

The Southern accent of the singers gave to the words a genuine, spiritual tone, mixing with the pure air of the forest and the countryside the appropriate place for a religious hymn.

"It's me . . . Oh Lord . . . It's me, Alleluia!"

"'Come to me . . . Oh, Lord . . . Come to me . . . "

"You set me free . . . Alleluia . . . You set me free!"

"At last, come to me . . . Alleluia . . . 0h Lord, Come to me . . . !"

THE END

Biography

Luis L Crespo, Sr. emigrated from Cuba after the communist revolution. He has a Public Accounting degree from University of Oriente. Mr. Crespo and family live in New England.